Howls of the Lost

Erin Jacobs

Aiiry Publishing Co.

Contents

this one is for the fated-mates lovers.

Fair warning: there is no smut to be had in this book.
Tension? Yes. Smut? No.
Not your thing? Totally understandable. But Logan and Torian
will be waiting for you if you ever decide you want something a
little lighter!

Chapter One

A SOFT BREEZE BLEW through the quiet woods, ruffling the white fur that covered my body.

Taking a deep breath to steady myself, I allowed every muscle to relax. Over the years, I had found that hunting required an immense amount of concentration. Opening my eyes, I exhaled and flicked my gaze over the small herd of deer around twenty feet away from where my pack and I were standing.

The others stirred restlessly behind me as I continued to watch the deer. Picking up on the noise, the largest buck raised his head and scanned the darkness of the trees concealing us.

"Would you guys shut up and stay still?" I thought to them as a low growl rumbled in my chest.

"Sorry, Tor," Ashlyn's smooth voice echoed in my head. Rolling my eyes, I glanced back at the three wolves behind me. They stared back at me, and Ashlyn's tongue lolled out the side of her mouth as she wagged her cream-colored tail.

My gaze traveled to David, my second, who lowered his head in acquiescence. *"Yes, Alpha,"* he said, his tone playful. He moved forward to bump his shoulder lightly against mine.

In return, I just rolled my eyes again.

Alpha.

We used the term loosely. For all intents and purposes, I *was* technically our Alpha. I was the one who kept us together, and the one they looked to when it came to the hard decisions. As Ashlyn moved to my side opposite David, I quietly sighed and faced the herd of deer once again.

"*On my signal,*" I said, preparing them for the attack. "*One, two, three. Go!*" Our muscles simultaneously released, and we sprang into the clearing.

Those poor animals never even saw it coming. Michael took down the largest buck while the rest of us picked off what we could. Ashlyn and David attacked a frightened doe together and my kill ended up being another buck. His neck snapped easily, and I was glad he experienced as little pain as possible.

Silence descended upon us as we ate. Being shifters, we could survive by hunting or taking on our human forms and eating normal food. For the past few months, however, we had kept ourselves continuously in wolf form. While there were other kinds of shifters in the world, most of the ones I ran into were lupine, like us. My knowledge of my kind was slim outside of the basics, because I had, unfortunately, never paid much attention to shifter history.

After a while, we had eaten our fill, and we stood. My gaze roamed over the other three wolves. We might have been a small pack, but they were the best and my only family. Ashlyn and Michael were mates, lucky to have found each other despite everything, so our family was due to grow before too long. David and I were simply counting down the days until they added a fifth little wolf to our pack.

The blood streaked through their muzzles finally caught my attention, alerting me to the fact that we should probably clean up. I closed my eyes to focus on my hearing. As I let it range out, I caught the trickling of a stream not far off in the distance.

"*C'mon,. Let's wash this off,*" I said as I turned in the direction the sound was coming from. They needed no further encouragement before we took off at a dead sprint.

The trees blurred together the faster we ran. As the wind continued to blow through my fur, my eyes fluttered closed again. That feeling was one that would never grow old. My pounding footfalls against the ground matched the pace of my heart, and everything else in the world fell away. The wind had an almost calming effect on the heightened senses that came with being a shifter.

Crack.

My body immediately fell to a standstill. The others slowed to a stop around me as my gaze raked over the surrounding woods. "*Go ahead,*" I told them, continuing to watch the trees as I backed up. "*I'll be right there.*"

David blankly stared at me. "*Torian, we're not leaving you.*"

"*I'll be fine,*" I growled out, irritation slipping into my voice. His older brother mentality tended to come out whenever he was worried about my safety, even though it was *my* job to worry about him.

"*Tor...*"

"*Just go,*" I ordered, fighting with everything I had to restrain my Alpha command. The one thing that would strip them of their free will and force them to follow out my orders. It was something I tried to avoid at all costs.

After sending skeptical glances my way, the three wolves finally complied and ran off. Once I was sure they were gone, I huffed and turned in the opposite direction. There was something, or someone, out there with us, and I was determined to find out what it was.

Time passed slowly as I sniffed through practically every bush surrounding the small area. Ready to give up, I shook out my coat and trotted off after the others.

Crack.

The sound of another twig snapping caught my attention just before something tackled me. I went airborne before my spine collided with the trunk of a tree, causing me to crumple into a heap at the bottom. Growling, I stood on shaky legs and faced my assailant.

The blood-red eyes of a vampire stared back at me.

That fact alone was enough to alert me he was freshly turned. Vampires' eyes stayed red for the first few months before they faded back to their natural color. Had his eyes not have been enough to convince me, the way his arms twitched along with his irregular breathing pattern would have. He was the stereotypical newborn that I had grown to hate. All ravenous instinct, no thought or planning. His blonde hair was dirty and disheveled, sticking up at random angles.

His rabid snarl echoed in the silence, and my own low growl mingled with his. As I advanced on him, my growl increased in volume until it was reverberating off the trees in one continuous strand. The slightest flicker of intimidation flashed in his crimson eyes, but it was gone as quick as it came. With slow and deliberate steps, I inched closer to him. It didn't take long before he leapt at me and I met him in the air.

When we crashed to the ground, a horrific *snap* bounced around the woods. My startled and pain-filled yelp mixed with the vampire's scream of agony, but I forced myself back onto my feet. He tried to stand as well, but his leg contorted at an awful angle. Noticing his injury, I used it to my advantage. Squeezing my eyes shut, I willed sinew, bone, and muscle to shift as I took on my human form. His quiet whimpers fell on deaf ears as I stalked to a nearby tree and ripped a limb free. Not caring that I was completely bare, I advanced.

He looked up at me through fear-filled eyes as I raised the make-shift stake above my head. "Rot in hell," I hissed out as I plunged it into his heart, killing him the only way I knew how. A screech escaped him as his pallor changed from pale ivory to stormy gray. Within a matter of seconds, there was nothing left of the newborn but a pile of ash.

Shifting back to wolf form, an uneasy feeling greeted me. My stomach immediately rolled. Something was wrong with my pack. They were too far away for me to hear them, but they were my responsibility. It was my job to protect them. And everything in me knew they needed me.

I ran.

Logan Gray cursed silently as the timber wolf from his pack pinned him to the ground. "*Rikki,*" he growled at her. Training with her had been a bad idea, and Logan knew it. She never fought fair.

As she pulled back, she flashed him a wolf grin. "*So sorry,*" she told him, sarcasm layering her words.

He stood and looked around at the four wolves he had with him. They were each immersed in their own thoughts, and Logan had to fight the urge to tackle his younger brother, Dalton. The only other black wolf in the clearing.

Logan met his brother's eyes and motioned the other wolf over. "*Dalton, your turn,*" he said.

Dalton trotted toward Logan, rearing for a chance to win a sparring match against his brother. It was one of their ongoing bets to see who could win the most fights in a month. A grin twisted Logan's lip as he lowered himself into a crouch. They were just about to begin their fight when the rapid cracking of twigs caught the attention of both wolves. Logan growled low in his throat as he turned to the opposite side of the stream.

The others jumped into the clearing with grace. There were three of them: one female and two males. The newcomers noticed him and his pack as they slowed to a standstill. The brown wolf was huge, and it stood to reason that he would be the small pack's Alpha, if they had even appointed one.

"*State your purpose,*" Logan ordered, his Alpha command laced through his voice. It would have no effect on them, but it would establish him as the territory head.

The brown wolf nodded as he spoke back to Logan. "*Just passing through,*" he said, his voice calm. "*We'll clean up and be on our way.*"

Only at the mention of cleaning did Logan notice the blood that marred all three of their coats. It only put him on higher alert. As he spoke again, a horrible screaming tore through the clearing. The nomadic pack exchanged worried looks before staring over their shoulders in the direction the sound had come from. Logan had to growl in order to regain their attention.

"*You are trespassing on my pack's territory,*" he said, his voice taut. The last time a nomadic pack had crossed through these lands, it had been a bloody fight. He didn't want a repeat. "*There are rules.*"

"*Puh-lease,*" the small cream-colored female muttered.

"*What was that?*" Logan snapped at her.

"*I said–*" she started, only to be cut off by the supposed Alpha.

"*Ash, hush,*" he told her.

"*Don't tell me what to do,*" she retorted.

Logan couldn't help but watch them in amazement. It was a rarity among their kind for a wolf to snap at their Alpha like that.

"*You'd be wise to listen to your Alpha,*" Logan said.

"*Michael? Alpha?*" she asked, snickering. "*Are you really that stupid?*"

Was she mocking him?

"*Then who is your Alpha?*" he asked, trying his hardest not to snap at her again. They had seemed cordial so far. There was no need to escalate the situation.

As if on cue, a new wolf swept its way into the clearing. The white wolf surveyed the scene before her, her crystal-blue eyes glittering with curiosity as she immediately sought Logan out.

"*I am,*" she said, her voice firm.

No sooner had the words reached Logan than something inside him awakened. The force of the single word echoing through his brain nearly forced him to the ground.

Mine.

Logan had finally found his mate.

"*Excuse me?*" he asked as realization finally dawned on him. She was the Alpha? That was impossible.

She limped over to the other three and her injury distracted Logan. Once she was standing in front of her pack, she turned to glare at him. Her eyes held no fear, and she emanated power and authority.

"*I am the Alpha of this pack,*" she stated. Sure enough, that was an Alpha's command coating her words.

Logan couldn't believe it. He had never heard of such a thing. "*A female Alpha?*" he questioned.

"*Yes,*" she answered with a roll of her eyes. "*A female Alpha.*" The condescension in her voice was almost palpable.

Her attitude caused his temper to spark, mate claim be damned. "*You are on my land. Have some respect,*" he stated, sinking into a hunting crouch.

"*I'll do what I please,*" she said, mimicking his position.

He launched himself across the stream without a second thought and landed directly in front of her, teeth bared. Her eyes widened in shock as she met his gaze, but her dark scowl was back in place so fast Logan thought he might have imagined it. She took a step toward him, only to wince when she placed pressure on her hind leg. Logan heard her teeth grind together as she prepared herself to attack, but one of her pack stopped her.

"*Torian,*" the tawny wolf, who had been quiet until now, said in a clipped tone. "*You're hurt. Fighting him right now is going to be useless. Please don't let your stubbornness make you injure yourself any more than you already have.*"

"*I can take care of myself, David,*" she snapped, tearing her eyes away from Logan.

"*I know that,*" he told her as his eyes gained a faraway look. "*But I'm not about to risk losing you again.*"

Her features softened as their gazes met. "*Dave...*"

"*Tor, don't,*" he said with an air of finality. Logan blinked at the exchange that had taken place. She was his Alpha, not the other way around.

"*Alright.*" Her soft voice broke Logan from his thoughts. "*Let's go,*" she said, glancing at Logan briefly before turning her back to him.

Absolutely not.

"*You're not leaving,*" Logan said.

"*Watch me,*" she retorted, not even bothering to turn around.

"*Let me rephrase,*" he said, running to stand in her path. "*You can't leave.*"

"*And why not?*" she asked, trying to step around him. Every time she made a move, Logan had already positioned himself to block her. A low growl rumbled in her chest as she looked up into eyes.

He melted under her gaze, all of his irritation fell away. "*You're injured,*" he reminded her. "*I won't let you leave just so it can get worse."* Or at least that was the excuse he was giving her. Truthfully, Logan just didn't want to watch his mate walk out of his life the minute he had found her.

Torian sighed in frustration and tried to move around him once again. She didn't succeed. *"I'll be fine,"* she growled, exasperation clear in her tone. *"Why do you care, anyway?"*

"Tor," David interjected, his eyes bouncing back and forth between the two Alphas. *"Maybe he can help."*

"I don't need his help."

"We have a pack doctor that can assess how bad it is," Logan threw out. nodding toward the hind leg she was still favoring.

"No."

"Torian," her pack chorused, sounding like this wasn't the first time they'd had an argument like this.

She winced. *"I hate you guys. You know that, right?"*

The cream wolf walked forward and nudged the white wolf with her shoulder. *"We know,"* she murmured.

The large brown wolf Logan had originally mistaken for the Alpha crouched low in front of Torian. *"Get on,"* he told her.

"Really, Mike?" she asked, staring at him.

"Really, Tor," he mocked in a horrible imitation of her voice.

With a reluctant sigh, she positioned herself on top of his back and once he stood, the brown wolf faced Logan. *"Lead the way,"* he said.

Logan nodded before turning and wading through the stream, with the nomadic pack following closely behind. His gaze fell on his pack, and he realized they were watching the other pack with apprehension. *"C'mon, guys,"* he called to gain their attention. *"We're going home."*

The small gray wolf curled her lip. "*You're bringing them with us?*" Brooke asked. She had been in more of the territory brawls than he cared to count. He couldn't blame her.

"*Their Alpha is injured and they'll be staying with us until she feels she can lead them on.*"

"*I can lead them on now,*" Torian called, her voice causing him to stop in his tracks.

Rikki, being the pest she was, didn't miss the exchange. "*Finally met your match, Logan?*" she asked, her voice layered with faux innocence.

"*Keep your mouth shut,*" he warned her.

"*Yes, sir!*" she quipped before trotting on ahead.

Logan could already tell it was bound to be a long, interesting day.

Chapter Two

A MATE, I THOUGHT to myself, trying to fully comprehend the idea.

Years ago, I had accepted the fact that having a mate wasn't in the cards for me. I didn't even want it anymore, so why was this being thrown at me? Beyond that, why was I allowing myself to take their help?

Useless vampires.

A growl bubbled out of my throat as I realized that if it hadn't been for the fight with the newborn, we could have avoided the entire ordeal.

"*Something wrong, Tor?*" David asked, drawing me out of my thoughts.

"*No,*" I lied.

"*Torian...*" he chastised, seeing right through me.

"*We shouldn't be doing this,*" I admitted. "*You guys should have just let me heal on my own.*"

"*You would have just made it worse, Tor,*" Michael said.

"*Nuh-uh,*" I argued.

"*What happened anyway?*" David asked.

"*A newborn.*" Another growl slipped past my teeth.

Up ahead, I heard Logan's feral snarl. David's head swiveled in that direction, but his attention almost immediately returned to me. *"Why didn't you let us stay and help?"* he asked.

"I thought it would be something easy. Like a bear."

"A bear is not easy. You should have let us help," Ashlyn threw in, a grim tone to her voice.

"Shut up, Ash."

"You wouldn't be injured now, would you?" she retorted with a bitter laugh.

"Ashlyn..." I warned.

"Torian, face it," she snapped, turning to look me dead in the eyes. *"If you weren't so stubborn, you wouldn't get hurt half as much as you do. You don't have to do everything on your own. We can handle it. But now, we've had to accept outsider's help because I'm pretty sure your leg's broken."*

Trying to contain the growl of irritation that wanted to spill out, I turned to stare blankly in the opposite direction. Ashlyn had a point, and I knew it. Too often, I tried to keep them separate from any and all danger. No one had ever stopped to protect me, so it was the least I could do for the wolves who allowed me to lead them.

"Didn't want his help anyway," I muttered.

"I can hear you, you know," Logan called from his position ahead of us.

"Don't care," I said, placing my head between Michael's shoulders.

"Are you sure about that?"

"Someone please shut him up before I do," I grumbled.

Ashlyn faced forward. But I had seen the mischief in her eyes and my whole body tensed. If I knew Ashlyn, she was up to something.

Sure enough, once Logan had torn his gaze away from me, she trotted silently past his pack. They all stared at her, but made no move to stop her as she pounced on Logan. They fell to the ground, and he snarled at her. She shook her head and stepped on his muzzle. Slowly wagging her tail, she turned to me.

"*How's that?*" she asked, a playful edge to her voice.

"*Control your pack, ma vie,*" Logan spat.

"*Are you talking to me?*" I asked, eyebrows knitting together. Ma vie? What did that mean?

"*Yes,*" he replied.

"*Then what did you just call me?*"

"*Ma vie.*"

"*And that means?*" I ground out, annoyance with him mounting by the minute.

"*Guess you'll never know,*" he said with a shrug, even though Ashlyn was still holding him to the ground.

"*Tell me.*"

"*Call off your dog and I will,*" he told me, and I could practically hear the smile in his voice. Once I connected gazes with Ashlyn, she sighed but removed her paw from Logan's snout all the same. "*It's in French,*" he said as he stood and shook out his midnight black coat.

"*That's not telling me what it means.*"

"*Then you'll just have to figure it out on your own, ma vie.*" Anger seeped into my veins as we continued moving. Not only did I have to sort this whole mate business out, but I had to figure out what his pet name meant too? Shaking my head, I caught sight of a town up ahead. "*Welcome to Riverview,*" Logan called to us as he broke into a sprint, his pack close behind him.

"*Does he expect me to carry you while I'm running?*" Michael growled as the territorial pack vanished.

"*Mike?*" I asked as an idea came to mind. "*You love me, right?*"

"*What do you want?*" he asked, apprehension creeping into his voice as he tensed up beneath me.

"*Turn around and run as fast as you can in the opposite direction.*"

"*You're impossible,*" he grunted as he faced back the way we had come.

"*Don't you dare listen to her,*" David said as both he and Ashlyn stepped into Michael's path. "*She needs help.*"

"*And if we don't make sure she gets it now, she's just going to make it worse,*" Ashlyn added.

"*They've overruled you, Tor,*" Michael said, turning back to Riverview.

But I didn't want help, and I didn't want a mate.

There were two types of shifters in our world. Nomads, like us, who moved and traveled as much as we wanted. Then there were the territorial packs, like Logan's. They were exactly what they sounded like. Packs that owned and ran a territory. Most of them had held their positions for centuries, and they looked down on nomads. They saw us as weaker because we didn't have the strength to defend and hold a territory.

The reality of the situation was, for our own reasons, none of us *wanted* to stay in one place for too long.

Being tied down to one territory was not high on my list of things to accomplish, and that was all that having a mate would do. Logan would want me to stay with him and join his pack. That task alone would be next to impossible. I had embraced the Alpha blood that ran in my veins, and I wasn't too keen on giving it up.

It was who I was.

Once we arrived in the center of the town, my eyes found Logan. He looked mildly annoyed and I couldn't help but to take a bitter satisfaction in his irritation.

"*Are you all okay?*" he asked as his eyes raked over my pack and finally settled on me.

"*Yes, but she's on my back,*" Michael spoke up, and I could almost feel him rolling his eyes. "*If I would have run, she could have fallen off and made her injury worse.*"

The timber wolf from his pack snickered. "*Nice going, Logan,*" she teased.

"*Be quiet, Rikki,*" Logan ordered, a soft Alpha command ringing clear in his exasperated voice.

She glared at him, looking like she wanted to tell him off. Unfortunately, under her Alpha's orders, she was silenced. It wouldn't last long. He hadn't put much force into it.

But still.

"*Seriously?*" I asked.

"*What did I do now?*" Confusion pinched his brows together.

"*You just used an Alpha command for something as petty as that?*" I sneered. "*I feel so sorry for your pack.*"

He snarled as his eyes met mine. They were the strangest shade of teal. Like the color of cresting waves when the sunlight hit them.

"I'm really going to need to teach you some manners," he said.

"You can try," I taunted.

"You've got yourself a challenge, ma vie."

"Stop calling me that."

"I don't think I will," he said. *"Now shift back."*

"No," I told him as a low snarl ripped its way out of my throat. Shifting in front of my pack was one thing, but there was no need to be naked in the middle of the town square.

"You can have my shirt, Tor," David offered. Without another word, Michael turned around and walked back toward the woods.

"Thanks, Dave," I said, breathing a sigh of relief as understanding dawned on Logan's face.

"Anytime."

We all shifted once the dense thicket of trees covered us. The boys automatically reached down and untied the clothes that they kept tied around their ankles. Ashlyn and I really needed to take a page out of the boys' book. But then again, a t-shirt and shorts didn't hinder running as much as a t-shirt, shorts, underwear, and a bra would. David tossed me his shirt as Michael gave Ashlyn his, breaking me out of my wayward thoughts. Ashlyn and I slipped the boys' oversized t-shirts over our heads at the same time that they pulled on their shorts.

A sigh slipped out of my mouth as I stretched, making sure not to put too much pressure on my leg. It was actually a relief to be on two legs again. Shaking my head, I ran my fingers through my mocha hair and tried to pull a few of the tangles out. Ashlyn grinned when I faced her.

"Good to be back," she said, her ocean blue eyes catching the sunlight.

"Couldn't have said it any better," I told her.

Michael walked up behind her and wrapped his arms around her waist. "Did I ever tell you how good you look in my shirt?" he asked her before spinning her around and planting a kiss on her lips.

"Gross," I muttered.

Laughter erupted around me, and David hugged me tightly. He spun me around, and a light laugh broke loose from my throat. He squeezed me tighter before placing me on my feet.

When I hit the ground, I had to bite back a scream of agony at the shooting pain that ripped through my left leg. In replacement I let out a small whimper followed by a string of profanities. David held my shoulders to steady me and raised an eyebrow.

"Definitely broken," I ground out, glancing down at my leg.

"I'm so sorry, Tor," he said as his eyes widened. Within seconds, he had swept me back into his arms.

"It's fine," I said, playfully hitting his shoulder. A grin stretched his lips as we began walking, and a knot formed in my stomach.

What was I going to do? I knew my pack wouldn't let me leave Riverview until I healed, but what would they do if they found out Logan was my mate? Would they fight me to stay? They all believed wholeheartedly in the mating claim, and I didn't think they'd see my side of things in the end.

The sound of voices carried to me and I glanced to where we had left Logan and his pack. My entire body froze as I took in the man that had to be Logan. His dark brown hair curled slightly over his forehead, leading directly to that set of piercing eyes that were focused solely on me. The slight stubble that adorned his chin gave him a ruggedly handsome look. And it was all I could do to force my eyes to move on. Like David and Michael, he wore only a pair of shorts, giving me a full view of his sculpted chest.

I swear, male physique was in the shifter genes.

Even in the way he stood, he was the very image of authority.

An Alpha through and through.

The silence surrounding us was deafening, and all eyes soon fell on me. More than almost anything else, I hated being the center of attention. An odd aversion for a leader, but nothing about my being Alpha was normal. I curled farther in to David's chest. He could sense my discomfort and he gave me a reassuring squeeze. Looking up into his eyes, I could feel myself calm. Having been together for so long, it was second nature for him to relax me.

Hell, half the time he was the only one that could.

Logan broke me out of my thoughts. His arms extended to David, an obvious request for him to hand me over. David started to comply, and I glared up at him before tugging on his hair.

"No," I said, my voice cutting through the silence. "I'm staying right here."

"Ma vie, come on," Logan said, rolling his eyes as he reached for me again. His voice was just as rough in his human skin as it had been when it echoed in my head for the first time. When he was within range, I smacked his hand. He snapped it back and shook it to relieve the pain.

David chuckled and went to hand me over to Logan again. "Don't you dare," I snarled at my best friend.

"C'mon, Tor," he said with a sigh. "He won't bite you."

"He's not touching me," I replied, my voice firm. "I'd much rather just cut my leg off." I didn't know where all the hostility was coming from, but I would bet it had something to do with the fact that my leg was broken.

At least that's what I was blaming it on.

Logan's growl rumbled around the square, and then he removed me from David's arms. Shrieking in defiance, I struggled to break free of Logan's iron grip without letting the shirt ride up my thighs.

Unfortunately, the task was impossible.

"You're just going to injure yourself more, ma vie." Logan's breath washed across my neck as he whispered in my ear.

"I don't care," I said, acid dripping off every word as I still attempted to escape his grip. His hold tightened even more as he carried me further and further away from my pack.

"Torian," he said my name sternly, yet softly, and my body stilled against my will. He chuckled. The sound was deep and rich, and I could feel myself relaxing into him. Stupid shifter hormone. My gaze lowered to the ground as I jutted my lower lip out into a petulant pout. "Look at me, ma vie," he cooed. I didn't want a mate, and I wouldn't allow myself to fall under this arrogant Alpha's spell. Logan leaned down until his lips met the shell of my ear. "C'mon. Look at me, Torian."

Sighing, I relented and met his gaze. "What do you want?" I asked, trying to control my voice and ignore the fact that I could feel his bare chest against me.

His eyes sparkled as his lips curled into a smirk. Finally realizing we had come to a stop, I looked around the room we were in. It had to be his. The walls were a simple dark blue, and the carpet was cream. A king sized bed held up residence on the right wall and a desk in the corner held a laptop. Two doors besides the one we came in lead to what I was guessing to be a bathroom and a closet.

He interrupted my scrutiny of the room by laying me down on the bed and positioning himself close to me, careful not to hit my leg.

"You," he said in a voice as soft as velvet.

Sitting up, I shoved him away from me. "Too bad," I said.

"You have realized we're mates, right?" he asked with irritation clear in his voice.

"Of course I have. That doesn't mean you control me, or that I have to accept it."

He looked taken aback. Dumbfounded. "Why wouldn't you want to?"

I picked myself up from the bed, but Logan gently pushed me back down. "I don't see how that's any of your concern," I growled.

"Obviously, since you are my *mate,* it automatically becomes my concern."

As I tried to get up again, Logan just pinned me to the bed with his weight. He had my wrists securely in his grip as he hovered over me.

I could feel it then, the bond that wanted to be accepted. It coiled beneath my skin, straining for him. And to Logan's credit, he kept his distance. Even though I could see the war raging in those teal eyes. It would be so easy for him to lower himself so that our bodies were flush together. But he didn't. He had me firmly secured, and that was it.

"Let me go," I said in a low voice. The feeling of being helpless was not one that I ever entertained.

"Your leg is *broken*. The town doctor is on his way here now to set it so it can heal faster," he said.

Irritation finally won out, and I kicked him in his balls with my good leg. He curled into himself with a groan as I shoved him onto the floor. "I still don't see why I have to stay here with *you*," I muttered while doing my best to get to my feet. Raising myself into a suitable standing position, I hobbled toward the door. Faster than I thought possible, he was up and in front of me, blocking my escape.

"You're staying here with me because we are *mated*," he stated, his voice fierce. "Don't you want that?" he asked, searching my face. When I made no move to answer, he sighed and changed the subject. "I'm sure you'll be on bed rest for a few days while you heal, but then you can move around again." His voice had morphed into a soothing tone, but it wasn't doing anything to cool my temper.

Taking a deep breath, I tried to calm myself and control it, anyway. "I obviously don't give a damn that we're mated, but fine. I'll allow the doctor to do whatever he needs." Falling back on the bed, I swung my legs up, wincing when my broken one knocked into the footboard. "Can you do me one favor?" I asked, trying, and probably failing, to make my voice sound sweet.

Logan raised his eyebrows at me. "What's that?"

"Clothes," I said. Being in nothing more than a long t-shirt while I was alone in a room with him was unnerving.

Without a word, he disappeared inside the closet for a minute before returning with a pair of shorts. "They're the smallest ones I have. They'll have to do," he said, tossing them to me and then turning his back to me.

Blinking uncertainly at his back, I shook my head. Not sure what I had been expecting, but chivalry wasn't at the top of the list.

"Thank you," I said as I pulled the shorts on. Relieved to be fully dressed, I sagged back against the pillows. "I'm gone the minute I fully recover," I grumbled under my breath.

A smile twisted his lip as he came over and sat next to me. The death glare that I aimed at him gave him the good sense to scoot a few inches away. "We'll see," he murmured cryptically, relaxing back against the headboard.

Dread twisted my stomach. I didn't trust that smile for the life of me.

Chapter Three

THE CEILING OF LOGAN'S bedroom had become incredibly interesting over the past hour. My leg only needed to be wrapped, but I still had to stay off of it for three days before it would completely heal. At least being a shifter was good for one thing. We healed fast.

The only bad thing?

I had to stay on bed rest in Logan's room, because he said there were no other available rooms.

I called bullshit.

If I didn't kill him, it would be a miracle. My eye was already beginning to twitch, and I had only been around him for an hour. Not that I didn't enjoy the company. It was just that I didn't particularly like *his* company.

"Ma vie, your eye is twitching," Logan pointed out, tracing a finger across my cheek.

"I wonder why that is."

"Why?"

"Probably because there is a certain annoying mutt sitting on my bed," I snapped, attempting to hit him.

A slow smile spread across his face as we both realized he was lying just out of reach of my arm. "Sorry to break it to you, but this is *my* bed."

"Not while I'm in it. It's not."

"Yes, technically, it still is."

Turning my head, I met his gaze. "Logan, if you are any kind of gentleman, you will respect my wishes and sleep on the floor while I'm here," I said in the sweetest voice I could manage.

"Alright, ma vie. I'll sleep on the floor," he relented, faster than I had thought he would.

Offering him a small smile, I turned my attention back to the ceiling. "Thank you."

Suddenly, I heard a bunch of elephants tramping into the room.

Alright, elephants may have been an exaggeration, but seven anxious shifters soon filled up the small room. The doctor must have finally given them the okay to come bug me.

The four from Logan's pack stayed close to the door, but Ashlyn, Michael, and David all came to my side. My gaze never strayed from the ceiling, despite the now incessant chatter, mostly coming from Ashlyn.

"What're you looking at, Tor?" David asked me, moving my hair out of my face as he knelt beside the bed.

A slight smile tilted my lips upward. "A panda in a tutu riding a giraffe in a zebra shirt, who's balancing on a—No, I'm pretty sure I'm just looking at the ceiling."

David just rolled his eyes and ruffled my hair. "Hilarious."

"I know, right?"

He poked my cheek. "So, how are you holding up?"

A sigh slipped out of my mouth. "Bed rest for three days. And I have to serve it *here*." I hooked my thumb in Logan's direction. "With *him.*"

"I think you'll survive. We'll come visit you every day," he said, chuckling.

"Yeah," Ashlyn threw in. "Wouldn't want you to have to deal with him all by yourself."

Logan's irritated growl caused me to stifle a giggle. Someone else in the room didn't succeed as well as I did. "Rikki, shut up," he told the redheaded girl from his pack. "And you," he said, pointing to Ashlyn. "I'd appreciate if you'd stop with the remarks about me."

Ashlyn sneered. "No."

This time I couldn't hold it in and a small laugh bubbled out of my mouth. Logan scowled at me, and I just shrugged. The redhead snorted, and his head whipped toward her.

"Rikki," he said, letting out a long-suffering sigh.

She laughed and lightly smacked his shoulder. "Oh hush. It's just fun."

"Hi, Rikki. I'm Torian. I like you already," I said, stretching across Logan to shake her hand.

She took my hand and grinned. "Ashlyn said you would."

The shifter in question shrugged when I shot her a curious look. "We talked outside," she explained.

Looking back at Rikki, I saw she was intently watching a point beyond me. Following her gaze, I noticed David was looking into her eyes with the same intensity.

Mated, I thought.

The elation for David coursed through my veins in an instant, but a somber feeling swiftly replaced it. He had waited so long for his mate to come along, and I would miss him when I left. Because I'd never ask him to give up the bond I had every intention of rejecting.

My hand reached over of its own accord and pulled at his hair. "Finally met your match, Dave?" I asked.

He blushed and looked away. Biting my tongue barely contained the 'aww' I wanted to spill when he said, "Shut up, Tor."

My excited clapping ended up gaining the attention of every person in the room. David rolled his eyes at me, a smile playing across his face. I just shook my head at him. Turning to Rikki, I narrowed my eyes at her. "You take good care of him. Got it?"

She blinked and let what I had said sink in. When it registered, she blushed and looked at the ground. "Thanks for the announcement, Torian," she muttered, raising her head and giving me a playful glare.

A cheeky grin overtook my face. "Anytime. And Tor or Tori is just fine." I looked past Logan to the three shifters I was clueless about. "Are you going to introduce us?" I asked him, nodding toward his pack.

He smiled and nodded, pointing to the blonde in the corner. She looked skeptical about the newcomers in the room. Her mouth was firmly closed as her eyes met and held mine. "That's Brooke. She's a little antisocial at the moment because she doesn't like new people, but she'll come around." He pointed to the male behind her. He was tall, but lithe. If I didn't know better, I would've assumed he was human at first glance. "That's Troy, her mate. He's the quiet one. You already know Rikki," he said, scowling at her. Troy smiled at me and waved as Logan pointed to the last person.

The boy's hair was shaggy, and with his angular features he looked strikingly like Logan. Except for his eyes, which were dark blue. He grinned at me and ambled over to the bed. Logan rolled his eyes when I gingerly shook the boy's hand. "And this is my little brother, Dalton. You can pretty much ignore him."

"Jeez, Logan. Be a little more inconsiderate, why don't you?" Dalton said, a frown pulling down the corners of his lips.

"Did I mention his sarcasm problem?"

I winked. "I think we'll be real good friends."

Dalton pumped his fist in the air. "Eat it, Logan! Your mate likes me more than you," he said, sticking his tongue out.

My stomach bottomed out as his words sank in.

How did he know I was Logan's mate? Had Logan told him?

I hadn't even told my pack, and now it was out in the open before I had prepared.

Logan punched Dalton in the arm and rolled his eyes, turning to me. "Your turn to do introductions."

Facing our small pack, I forced a smile to conceal my unease. "That's Ashlyn; I'm sure you've noticed she can't keep her mouth shut." I motioned to Michael. "Michael, our muscle man, and Ash's mate." I winked at him as he rolled his eyes at me. Finally, I pointed to David. "And *this* is David. He's just well..." I trailed off, and he raised an eyebrow as I shrugged. "He's David."

He mock punched my arm. "Thanks so much, Tor."

"Torian?" Brooke called, gaining my full attention. "You're their Alpha, right?"

"Yes," I said.

She came over and sat at the foot of the bed. "How's that possible? It's obviously true. I could hear it in your voice when you announced yourself. I've just personally only ever heard of male Alpha's."

My body tensed. I really didn't want to answer that question. David and Logan noticed my anxiety, and they each laid a hand on my shoulder. Relaxing a little, I forced out another fake smile. "It's a long story... let's just say it runs in the family."

Brooke gave me a small smile. She obviously wanted more than that, but she took my hint and didn't press the subject further. My pack all knew my history, but it had been a while before I confided in them. Logan's pack was all new to me, and I probably wouldn't be comfortable enough to tell them my story for a while.

If ever.

Logan poked me in the side, and I jumped. Luckily, I didn't mess up anything with my leg, but I turned to frown at him. "What was that for?"

"You zoned out there for a bit, ma vie."

Scowling, I chucked a pillow at him. He let it smack him right in the face and I let out a short laugh. Turning my head, I glanced out the window. To my bewilderment, I saw stars twinkling back at me. When had it gotten to be so late?

As if on cue, a yawn escaped me.

"Alright guys, file out. Torian needs her sleep," Logan said, softly chuckling.

"Love you guys," I called to my pack as they left. They echoed in back in unison before walking out.

Snuggling down into the covers, it only mildly shocked me to feel the bed dip beside me.

"Floor, Logan," I ordered in a soft voice.

"Aw. C'mon," he whined. Opening one eye, I saw him pouting, an irresistible puppy-dog face adorning his features. I scowled at him.

"How'd you know I can't resist puppy-dog faces?" I asked.

"Good guess, apparently," he said, grinning as he slipped under the covers next to me. Slowly, he dared to snake an arm around my waist.

"Get on your own side of the bed or I'll rip your arm off," I murmured, not sounding the least bit threatening.

"You'll accept me one day, ma vie," he commented, his deep voice causing a shiver to slide down my spine.

"Stop calling me that. It's not likely."

I could almost feel his smirk in the darkness. "I like it, *ma vie*. And it's a promise, you'll fall for me. Our mating wasn't a mistake."

"In your dreams," I whispered around a yawn.

Torian was asleep just after she spoke, so she never heard Logan's soft, "Every night now, Torian." Nor did she feel him scoot closer and pull her against him as he fell asleep as well.

Chapter Four

WHEN I WOKE UP, it took everything I had not to groan out loud. There was no way I wanted to be awake. In my half-asleep stature, I cuddled closer to the solid form radiating heat beside me. Sighing, my entire body relaxed as I began to fall back asleep.

The slight rumbling beneath me was what snapped me back to reality.

Ever so slowly, I opened my eyes. I had nuzzled into the crook of Logan's neck, and I drew back to look up at him. He was already gazing at me, an ear-to-ear smile adorning his face. Scowling, I pulled away from him. Instead of letting me go, Logan constricted his arms around me like a vise.

Sighing, I slumped back down with a huff. "I thought I told you to stay on your side of the bed," I grumbled.

"Did I happen to mention I'm not very good at following orders?" he asked.

"No."

"Well then, I'm not very good at following orders." A small laugh escaped him before he could catch it.

"You're infuriating."

He didn't even try to control his laughter this time. The sound was warm, and it caused a slight fluttering in my stomach that I wasn't particularly fond of.

"I can't help it, ma vie."

The irritation that his little pet name for me caused was irrational, but it was probably because I didn't know what it meant. For all I knew, he could be calling me some filthy name. Blowing my hair out of my face, I tried wriggling free again.

"Could you let go?" I asked after a minute of fruitless attempts at escape.

"Magic word?"

"Please?" I muttered.

"What was that?" Logan cupped his ear and leaned closer, feigning a hearing impairment.

"Please!" I all but yelled.

Logan cringed, but unwrapped his arms from around me all the same. "Was that so hard?"

Deciding to ignore him, I turned onto my side so that I was facing away from him. Silence descended upon the room, and it wasn't exactly uncomfortable. In fact, as I listened to the steady rhythm of Logan's breathing, I slipped into sleep again.

Logan heard Torian's breathing change as she fell back to sleep. Carefully, he slipped out of bed and made his way toward the door. He knew Torian needed her rest in order for her leg to heal, so he decided he would get to know her pack better while she was recovering.

On the way down the hall, Logan glanced at the family pictures that lined the walls. Pictures of himself, as well as Dalton and their parents, were smiling back at him. He tried in vain to ignore the sporadic, empty places where pictures had been removed, but it was harder than he had expected. Before he could dwell too long in the past, Logan heard the chatter from the living room carry to him. Mentally shaking himself, he turned into the room with everyone else.

Rikki and Torian's Beta were deep in conversation in the far corner. Logan couldn't help the sad smile that graced his lips. He had always imagined finding his mate would be more like that. An instant connection that neither of them could deny. And while the connection was there, he couldn't fathom why Torian wanted nothing to do with it. He had so many questions for her, but he suspected she wouldn't give him many answers.

With an angry huff, Logan fell onto the couch next to Dalton. The younger brother turned with a smile. "Morning, Logan!" he chirped.

Rolling his eyes, Logan playfully punched Dalton's shoulder. "Why are you such a morning person?" he grumbled.

Dalton shrugged. "It's a gift."

"Yeah, sure."

"So, how bad did you irritate Tor last night?" Ashlyn called from where she sat with Michael.

Logan glanced in her direction and for a moment thought about ignoring her, but she was important to Torian. It would probably be best for him if Ashlyn didn't hate him.

"I think I fared pretty well," he finally said.

Ashlyn quirked an eyebrow at him, looking as if she had more to say. But she kept her mouth shut. For now, Logan wasn't important enough to bother with.

She was worried about Torian. How well was she handling everything? Ashlyn was starting to think forcing Torian to take Logan's help was a bad idea. Anyone with common sense could sense that they were mates. But Ashlyn feared Torian would completely reject the claim.

Ashlyn may not trust Logan just yet, but she wanted to see Torian happy. Her friend needed to stop running. For Torian's own good, Ashlyn just hoped she would at least give Logan a *chance.*

Sleeping so much was not normal for me. The pattern of Logan's ceiling had been forever branded into my brain from all the hours of staring at it I had been doing. Thoughts continued to swirl through my head with no certain course. Things I had filed away in a little black box at the very back of my mind started to rattle, threatening to break free and demand my attention. But I didn't want to dwell in the past. The memories I had locked away needed to stay there.

Which was one of many reasons I was having such a problem with the whole mating deal. Mates were supposed to know everything about one another. They were supposed to open up and trust each other, but my ability to trust was damaged. My past was where it was supposed to be, in the *past*, and I didn't want to end up drudging up old memories with Logan. Maybe he wasn't as bad of a guy as I had him painted in my head, but I didn't want to get close to anyone else.

What if history repeated itself?

The little black box rattled.

The creaking of the door caused me to throw myself back into the present and away from the recesses of my mind. David inched his way through the doorway, and when he saw I was awake, a broad smile overcame his face. He crossed the room, and with one look at him, I could tell he was straining to be easy as he lowered himself onto the bed. He obviously didn't want to risk bothering my leg. With his grin still in place, he reached for my hand and covered my icy fingers with his much warmer ones.

"How're you holding up, Tor?" he asked, concern flashing across his features.

I shrugged. "As well as anyone can be in this situation."

David's eyes tightened around the corners as he forced a smile. "You're not planning to give him any chance at all, are you?" he asked, his voice already resigned.

A sigh slipped past my lips. "You think I should." Knowing David as well as I did, I didn't even bother with trying to make it sound like a question. I knew what he was thinking.

"Of course you should. He's your *mate,* Tor. You really think he's going to hurt you?"

"Well..." I trailed off because David's tawny eyes were boring straight into mine. His protective side was making its annoying self known. "Maybe not intentionally."

"Part of being a shifter is accepting the mate claim, Tor. You're not complete without him. It's the way we work. You're really going to throw that away after being alone for so long?"

"I have my pack," I pointed out. He only stared at me in response. "What do you want me to do? I don't want this. I know that you've found Rikki and you'll want to stay but-"

"This is about *you*," he stated, cutting me off.

"And *I* don't care," I seethed. "A mate just really isn't in the cards for me. You know that the tradition is a male Alpha with a female Luna at his side. It's the way things have always gone, save for extenuating circumstances like a death. But I'm our Alpha. By choice. I'm not a Luna who's Alpha died to put me in this position. I've always accepted that was because I wasn't meant to have a mate. There must've been a mistake somehow."

David rolled his eyes at me. We both knew I was grasping at any blind excuse I could find.

"Quit lying to yourself, Tor. You're scared. You're genuinely scared for the first time since I've known you, and it's killing you." His voice was gentle, but it cut me like a knife.

Because he was absolutely right.

The thought of a mate terrified me. Hell, the thought of *any* long-term commitment scared me. That was part of why we were a nomadic pack.

If I couldn't even bring myself to face my own demons, how was I supposed to handle anybody else's?

Shaking myself, I brought my gaze back to David's. "How do you see right through me?" I asked.

The hint of a smile twitched at the corners of his mouth. "Because I'm the only one you've fully let in."

Grumbling unintelligibly under my breath, I sank back down into the covers. "Just drop it for now, okay? I'll be up and moving around soon and I'll make a definite decision then."

Unfortunately, from the look on his face, I knew David wouldn't be letting it go that easy. "Tor, what happened with your parents–"

A snarl rumbled deep in my chest before I could stop it. "Don't you dare try to bring them into this. That has nothing to do with what's going on."

"Don't even bother lying to me. We both know that they have *everything* to do with what's going on in that head of yours."

My jaw snapped shut with an audible *click*. "The subject is closed, David."

"Fine," he relented with a sigh.

"Really?"

"Really."

The grin that spread across my face couldn't really be helped. Staying angry with David was near impossible. "I hate you," I muttered as I shoved his shoulder.

"Hey," he said as he laughed. "It's not my fault that I'm so adorable you can't stay mad at me."

His added wink at the end of his sentence made me want to hit him again.

"Where's Logan?" I asked him, propping myself up on my elbow.

He shrugged. "I've been in here with you. How would I know?'

"Good point," I muttered, huffing. Why did I care anyway? It wasn't like I *wanted* to see the other male.

"Is someone missing her mate?"

"Not me." As soon as the words were out of my mouth, a loud yawn escaped me.

"Tired?"

"No," I replied too quickly.

David shook his head before pushing me down into the bed. "Get some rest, Tor."

"I've *been* getting rest."

"I know, but your leg needs all your energy to heal. You know that. It's not like this is your first broken bone or anything," he said, the smallest amount of bitterness lacing his voice.

"Don't remind me." I winced.

"Sleep," he demanded, already getting up to leave.

"Fine," I mumbled as he slipped out of the room.

Groaning, I rolled over to face away from the door. David acted like he was my father sometimes and though it got annoying after a while, I was still thankful for it. If it wasn't for him, I would probably never think of taking care of myself. My pack always came first.

But now I had a mate to worry about as well.

Why did we have to run into him? Sometimes I swore that whoever was up there controlling our fate had it in for me. Why else did I keep getting these kinds of curveballs thrown at me? My head throbbed from all the thoughts swirling around inside it. Maybe more sleep wasn't such a bad idea.

Chapter Five

Hours later, it was the sound of screaming that woke me up.

As I blinked my eyes open, I realized that my headache had never fully subsided. To say that the yelling wasn't helping it would be an understatement. Their voices stabbed through my brain repeatedly, causing me to squeeze my eyes shut and cover my ears to block out the sound.

It wasn't helping.

"You hit me!" I heard Ashlyn's unmistakable voice yell.

"That's the point!" That was Dalton's voice.

"No, it's a race!"

"Read the case," he snapped at her. "It says *Crash*. You're supposed to hit each other."

"He's right, Ash," David and Michael said in unison.

"No he's–"

"You're wrong, Ash. Give it up!" I hollered, cutting her off.

There was a beat of dead silence before I heard Rikki say, "I think we woke her up."

"No shit," I grumbled, rolling my eyes at the group.

Not even a minute later, a slender pair of arms wrapped around me. "I'm so sorry to wake you up. They're just so irritating," Ashlyn apologized in a rush.

"Its fine, Ash," I said, laughing and returning her hug.

From the sudden atmospheric change in the room, I knew he was there. I didn't even have to look to know that Logan was standing close. He was leaning against the doorframe, his teal eyes already trained on me. When our gazes met, he gave me a small smile before turning away from me. Sighing, I refocused on Ashlyn, who I realized had been talking.

"You haven't heard a word I've said, have you?" she asked, a small smile tugging at the corners of her mouth.

"No."

She sighed before shoving my shoulder. "I said, if you'll excuse me, I'm going to go kick Dalton's ass at this game." She got up from the bed and walked out of the room. When she drew level with Logan, she poked him in the chest to gain his attention. "If you do anything out of line, I'm coming back here to kick *your* ass for real." And with that, she flounced off down the hall.

Logan glared at her before turning back to me. "Your friend gets on my nerves," he muttered, pushing off the doorframe and coming farther into the room.

"Sorry," I said in a soft voice, my eyes trailing over him as he continued to make his way to the bed.

At least I could say that whoever controlled mates had been kind to me. Logan wasn't hard to look at. Even though he was wearing a loose t-shirt, his defined arms and torso were still clear.

As my eyes made their return trip back up, I saw the smug smile on his face.

He'd caught me. My face was instantly scarlet.

"Like what you see?" he asked as he sat down on the edge of the bed.

"Leave me alone," I snapped, my embarrassment still lacing my voice as I threw a pillow at his head. He easily dodged it.

"I don't think I will." He had the nerve to inch closer.

"What're you doing?" My entire body went rigid when he took my hand in his much larger one.

Logan started tracing patterns on the back of my hand. "Can I ask you something?" His voice sounded even deeper than usual.

"Sure." What was he up to?

"Do you hate me?" he asked, raising his head and piercing me with his gaze.

"Of course not. Why would you–"

"Think that?" he finished for me. "Maybe because I've finally found my mate, and she doesn't seem to want anything to do with me." His voice was bitter, and I couldn't blame him.

My heart pounded into overdrive as the guilt hit me square in the chest. He was hurt, and it was my fault. As much as I wanted to deny Logan, I couldn't fight the fact the connection that had already taken root. It was just one of many consequences of being mated.

"I'm sorry, Logan. I'm not cut out for having a mate. I'm sorry that you're the one that got stuck with me..." my voice trailed off and I tried to pull my hand away from him, but he just held tighter.

"Torian, look at me," he ordered, but his voice was soft. I just shook my head in response, turning even farther away from him. He needed to just let me go. He'd be better off. That much, I was sure of. "I said look at me," he repeated, his voice firmer than it had been as he placed a finger under my chin and forced me to meet his gaze. His eyes smoldered into mine as he cupped my cheek in his palm. "You're my mate, Torian. Let me make the choice of whether or not you're cut out for it."

His touch was radiating heat all the way through my body, warming me to the core.

"I can't," I whispered, feeling the treacherous tears welling up behind my eyes. The last thing I wanted to do was cry in front of him. "I don't want a mate."

His eyes searched mine. "What're you afraid of?" he questioned, his eyebrows drawing together and casting a deep shadow over his cheekbones.

"Nothing," I muttered, jaw clenching.

"You're scared of getting hurt," he said so matter-of-factly, for an instant I almost believed he could read my mind.

"How did you–" I started before I caught myself. Clearing my throat, I lowered my eyes. "How did you come up with that?"

"Nice try."

Damn.

Shaking my head, I pulled my face out of his grasp. "Please leave," I muttered.

"Why don't you trust me?"

"You haven't earned it."

"And how can I if you don't even give me a chance?" he pressed, voice raising the slightest bit. My eyes widened, and I shrank farther back into the bed. He sighed, pinching the bridge of his nose. "I'm sorry," he said after a beat or two of deep breathing.

I recognized the trick. It was one I had seen many times as a child. It was a calming technique.

I took my own deep breath to brace myself. Logan was his own person, not *her*.

"It's okay."

"It's not," he replied. "But thank you."

I nodded, relaxing back against the pillows again. I was more than happy to let the incident slip away.

He laid down beside me, almost touching but not quite. "I'll gain your trust, ma vie. I promise," he vowed.

"Not likely."

"Give me a *little* credit."

"I'll be gone before that ever happens," I muttered under my breath.

Even though I had kept my voice low, Logan apparently heard me all the same.

"Not on my watch," he said.

"Excuse me?" I asked.

"Do you really think I would willingly let you leave?"

"And how exactly do you plan on stopping me?" He just raised his brows at me. "Oh please. I could take you in my sleep."

He propped himself up on his elbow and leaned in close to me. "Is that a challenge, ma vie?" he taunted. I simply nodded in response. A smile curved his lips as he moved to my ear. "Bring it on."

My breath stalled as a series of shivers skittered down my spine. "Back off," I said, glowering at him.

He chuckled before doing as I asked and leaning back against his own set of pillows. "Just give this a chance."

"So where're your parents?" I asked. I could feel his gaze on my face, but I refused to look at him.

"They've been gone for a few weeks on vacation. It was their anniversary," he told me, thankfully going along with the conversation change.

"How come you're Alpha?" I wondered. While yes, I was a young Alpha, I was a nomad. The rules were a little different. A little more skewed. Logan was part of a territorial pack. Which meant his father should still be in charge.

"No real reason," he responded with a shrug. "Mom and Dad had Dalton and me late in life. By the time I was twenty, Dad was over being Alpha, so he asked me if I wanted to step up. Obviously, I agreed."

"How old *are* you?" I asked, turning to him with narrowed eyes. The question had been burning in my mind for a while now. He could be anywhere from late teens to late twenties with the way he looked.

"Twenty-four. Coming up on twenty-five in August." He turned to me and pierced me with those eyes of his. "What about you, Torian? How old is the female Alpha?"

"Freshly twenty-one." He studied me in a way that made me fidget. I didn't like being under his scrutiny.

"How long have you *been* Alpha?" he asked after a few beats of silence.

"Not sure." I told him, worrying my lip as I thought about it. "Little over five years, I guess."

Logan's eyes about popped out of his head.

"You've been an Alpha since you were *sixteen*?" he sputtered.

"Yes," I drawled. Was it really that big of a deal?

"Why?"

"Reasons," I answered in a clipped tone. I could all but feel myself shutting down. My heart constricted painfully at the thought of why I was on my own. The thought of opening up to Logan scared me almost as much as finding out I had a mate did. Thankfully, Logan seemed to realize I didn't want to talk about the situation.

I was quickly learning that having a mate was more terrifying than any vampire I had ever come across.

"You think she's going to be okay?" Ashlyn asked David as she sat down next to Michael on the couch.

"You know Torian. She's unpredictable. We're just going to have to wait and see," David replied as his eyes trailed to the far corner of the room where his own mate was sitting with the rest of Logan's pack.

"Well, do you think he's good enough for her?" Ashlyn snapped, her patience with the rest of her pack growing short.

Michael wrapped his arms around her and drew her close to him. "Ash, in your opinion, no one will ever be good enough for Tor," he said with a teasing edge to his voice.

She huffed indignantly before crossing her arms over her chest. "Well, you guys can't tell me you don't feel the same. You *know* how hard this must be on her. And we barely go back to see her, so she's just left in there with *him*." Her voice was strained as she thought about what her friend must be going through. But Ashlyn knew in her heart that she was right where she needed to be. They needed to let Torian and Logan have time to sort through this.

"I know that look, Ash," David said, narrowing his eyes at her.

"What?" she asked, batting her eyelashes in faux innocence.

"Don't you dare go back there," the boys said in unison.

Ashlyn glared at the pair. "You guys are no help," she grumbled.

Michael opened his mouth to answer, but stopped at the loud bang from down the hall. "Damnit, Logan!" came Torian's voice not even five seconds later.

The nomadic pack exchanged a quick glance before simultaneously bolting down the hallway. Nothing could prepare them for what they saw when they peeked their heads into Logan's room.

Chapter Six

WHEN THE OTHERS ARRIVED at Logan's door, I knew my face was crimson. As the feathers fell down around me, I glared with everything I had at Logan, who was still rolling with laughter. The sound was reverberating off the walls and making it extremely hard to stay mad at him.

"Tor?" David asked, trying to contain his own amusement.

"What?" I didn't bother taking my eyes off of Logan, who still hadn't settled down any.

"What happened?" David's eyes roamed over every inch of the feather-covered room.

"He hit me," I said, pointing at the other pack's Alpha, who finally seemed to sober up.

"Oh, c'mon now, Torian," Logan jeered, snagging me by the waist and carefully pulling me into him. He was so gentle about it he didn't jostle my leg in the slightest.

"Don't even start with me," I growled before turning to David. "It was him. I was apparently being *uncooperative*, so he figured it would be okay to throw a pillow at me. I threw one back, and then when he hit me again, it exploded."

The whole time I had been talking, I tried to escape Logan's hold. He just held me tighter the harder I fought.

"Calm down, ma vie," he murmured, speaking only loud enough for me to hear.

His voice seemed to trigger a reaction in me I wasn't very fond of. My body instantly relaxed and fell willingly into his warm embrace. Sighing, I admitted defeat to myself for the time being and nestled in closer to him. I could practically feel his smile as his arms relaxed until they were just resting across my abdomen. If I was being honest with myself, it was extremely comfortable. But I knew it could never last.

"Tor," Ashlyn called, drawing my attention to her.

"What?"

Her eyes narrowed at Logan and me, but she didn't comment. "How much longer do you think your leg has?" she asked.

"I should be able to get up the day after tomorrow," I said.

And freedom was right around the corner.

Logan tensed up beneath me as if he could read my mind.

"Why do you ask?" he directed his question at Ashlyn, but I knew he was on the same page as I was. Once the doctor cleared me, I had no intention of sticking around.

"Because I want to know when we're leaving."

My eyes traveled to David as Logan and Ashlyn bickered. He looked torn. He knew I was dead set on leaving, but his mate was here. And he actually wanted her. I would never ask him to leave her or for Rikki to leave her pack and come with us. Which only left one option.

David was going to stay here.

The thought brought tears to my eyes. He was like a brother to me. How was I going to function without him?

"Tor?" he asked just then, his tawny eyes raising to meet mine. When he saw I was on the brink of crying, he crossed to the bed and knelt in front of me. "Jesus, what's wrong?"

"Nothing," I muttered, shaking my head.

"I'm calling bullshit," he told me, forcing me to meet his eyes. "C'mon, tell me."

"Rikki's here," I said, my voice barely audible even to my own ears.

Realization dawned on his face as he rapidly shook his head. "That doesn't mean anything-"

"Stop. Of course it does. You've told me yourself that you want a mate more than anything in the world. It's okay."

Logan had been eerily silent the whole time, and he finally spoke up.

"You're *truly* planning on leaving?" he asked. His voice seemed to break slightly, and that alone was almost enough to make me change my mind.

Almost.

"Yes."

David gave me a sharp look, and his face said it all. He wanted me to at least make an attempt with Logan. But what if things crashed and burned? What was I supposed to do then?

"Challenge her," my Beta rushed out, eyes sparking as he turned his attention to Logan.

"What?" Logan asked at the same time I thought it.

David rolled his eyes. "She's an Alpha. Challenge her in a fight,"

My eyes widened as I realized what he was doing. He wanted Logan to issue a *challenge*? He knew full well that no self-respecting Alpha could back down from a fight, no matter the circumstances.

Which, I realized too late, was exactly what he wanted.

"I challenge you, Torian," Logan said before I could even open my mouth. "If you win, you're free to go. If I win, stay here for six months and make an honest attempt at this." His voice was firm and full of authority, laced with his Alpha's order.

The power of my own Alpha blood flared in my veins as I turned to meet Logan's eyes.

"Accepted," I agreed evenly, my Alpha tone infecting my voice even though I tried to keep it at bay.

"Good," he said, eyes sparkling with mischief.

"You're a traitor," I told David, turning to punch him in the arm.

"And I'm not sorry at all."

Ashlyn smacked him on the back of the head. "Now look what you've done."

Laughing softly, I looked back at Logan to see him already smiling down at me. "What?" I asked.

"Nothing, ma vie," he said, chuckling as he drew my body closer to his.

"Can you let go?" I asked. When he opened his mouth to refuse, no doubt, I cut him off. "So I can lie down."

He didn't look too happy about it, but he released me all the same. Offering a small smile, I laid down and carefully rolled onto my stomach.

"C'mon guys," I heard Ashlyn say as everyone filed out of the room.

"How are you feeling?" Logan inquired once the door was closed.

"Fine, I guess," I replied with a shrug, blowing a few feathers away from me. Warmth radiated out from the small of my back, and I realized it was because Logan had laid his hand there.

"Better?" he murmured, his hand slowly creeping higher until it rested between my shoulder blades.

"Significantly," I honestly answered. His touch was easing all the stress that had knotted the muscles in my body until it was nearly nonexistent.

He massaged my neck, and I had to bite back a moan at how good it felt.

"Can I ask you a question?" he asked after a while.

"It depends."

"Why are you so against having a mate?"

"Not that question," I said, tensing up again.

He shushed me. "Calm down. I won't force you to answer. I was just curious." He continued to knead my shoulders, not breaking for a moment.

"Stop trying to figure me out."

"You're going to lose the challenge, and then I'll have plenty of time to get inside that head of yours."

"*Or* I'll win and you'll be forced to watch as I leave," I fired off. His arrogance was infuriating. Why was he so sure he was going to win? I had been alone for years before finding my pack, and there was a reason I had lived through them. I honed my skills from nothing more than my primal instinct of survival.

Memories stirred as my mind retreated to my first days on my own. The fear had been almost enough to tip me over the edge into insanity, but I refused to give *them* the satisfaction of it. I pushed through and made it on my own. If there was one thing I was going to ensure, it was that I didn't die.

Eventually, I found David. We found Ashlyn soon after, and then Michael. We did okay for a while, but it didn't take long before the Alpha blood in my veins began boiling. Demanding that I acknowledge it. Revel in it.

"Torian?" Logan called, breaking through my reverie.

"Huh?"

"Where did you go?"

I debated telling him, but then thought better of it. What good would it do? I didn't want his pity and I sure as hell didn't need it.

"Leave it alone," I finally told him, realizing he was still waiting for an answer.

"Alright." He sighed.

"Thank you."

"You know you *can* confide in me, right?" he asked after few moments of silence.

So much for dropping the subject.

"Logan–"

"Stop," he said, voice quiet but still firm. "Just stop trying to push me away because it won't work. Remember how you said David wants a mate more than anything? I'm the same way. I've waited my whole life to find you. Do you know how hard it was to step up as Alpha of a pack like this one without somebody to stand beside me? It was, and has been, absolute hell."

My heartstrings pulled for him. Of course I knew how being a mateless Alpha felt.

I was one.

You constantly felt empty, but for me, it was a necessary evil. I couldn't risk getting close to anyone else.

"I'm sorry," I finally said.

"Its fine." He sounded anything but fine.

"I know you can't possibly understand why this is so difficult for me. But please, just let it go. If you win this stupid challenge, we'll see how it goes from there."

"Alright," he agreed, laying down beside me.

A peaceful silence descended over the room. But with the silence came the memories. Flashbacks danced behind my eyes like a ticker-tape. These conversations with Logan were not helping to keep that little black box in the back of my mind sealed.

The next couple of days passed in a blur before Dr. Walker came back and told me my leg had fully healed.

Unfortunately, it was the day of the challenge. I heaved a heavy sigh before dragging myself out of bed. Logan was nowhere to be found, so I cautiously made my way toward the room I had figured out was the bathroom. Just as I was about to go in, I realized I didn't have clothes to change into. Cursing under my breath, I turned and went out into the hallway.

I knew that turning left would lead me to the kitchen and living room area, so I took my chances and wandered to the right.

I was just hoping I would run into one of the girls. Thankfully, Rikki stepped out of the third door down from Logan's.

"Thank gods," I exclaimed.

"Torian!" she yelped, jumping slightly. "Don't sneak up on me like that!"

"Sorry." I bit down on my lip to stop myself from smiling.

"You're fine," she said, laughing. "You look lost, though. Can I help you with something?"

"Yeah. I want to take a shower, but I don't have any clothes. Could I borrow a few things?"

"Of course!" She grabbed my hand and towed me back into her room. She didn't wait for any kind of response before she disappeared inside her closet. While she was gone, I took the time to study her room. The set up was similar to Logan's. There was a queen bed shoved into the corner closest to me, a desk on the far wall with a laptop on top of it, and a dresser holding a massive stereo system standing next to the desk. The bedspread and walls were red, and the cream carpet was soft as cashmere under my feet.

"Nice room," I called to her as I moved to sit on the bed.

"Thanks," she said, appearing right in front of me. "You can have these," she continued, thrusting a wad of fabric into my hands.

"Thanks?"

"No problem." She waved me off.

"Well, I'll see you in a bit." I stood and headed to the door.

"I'll tell Logan you're up," she said, walking out into the hall with me.

She brushed past me and made her way toward the kitchen. When she disappeared around the corner, I winced. I wanted to avoid Logan at all costs, not alert him to the fact that I was awake. Sighing, I shoved his door open and wasted no time getting to the bathroom. I tossed the clothes Rikki had given me onto the counter and stripped out of David's t-shirt and Logan's shorts that had been on my body for far too long.

The hot water washed away all the dirt and grime that came from being in wolf form for too long as I stepped under the spray. I used Logan's shampoo and after I had washed my hair and body, I just stood under the water and let it unknot all the muscles in my back. I stayed there until the water ran cold and then wrapped a towel around myself before stepping up to the vanity.

Bracing myself, I wiped my hand across the mirror to remove the steam build-up. The girl looking back at me was exactly like I had expected. My blue eyes showed my exhaustion, and I had lost some of the tan I had gained while we were in the south. Blowing out a breath, I pushed away from the traitorous mirror and grabbed the pile of clothes, examining what they were. She had given me a pair of leggings, a soft, flowy t-shirt, and a pair of underwear.

I tossed the towel over the shower curtain rod and slid into the clothes. After dressing, I went through Logan's drawers in search of a brush. The best I could come up with was a comb, so I pulled it through my hair until most of the tangles were gone. Setting the comb back in the drawer I had found it in, I decided it was time to face the music.

Stepping out into Logan's bedroom, I fully debated the merits of just crawling back into bed. Logan wouldn't care. In fact, he'd probably be happy.

But I knew I couldn't do it. More than anything, I needed to get out of this town.

And the only way to do that was to beat Logan in this fight.

Chapter Seven

THE FIRST PERSON I noticed when I walked into the kitchen was Logan. His eyes snapped to mine the minute I breezed into the room, and then I took in the others. Rikki, Dalton, and David were all scattered around.

"Morning," I said right next to David's ear as I came to a stop beside him.

He jumped, knocking his hand into his coffee cup and causing it to slosh onto the white countertop. "Jesus, Tor! Don't do that!" He placed his hand over his heart. With my advanced hearing, I heard as it beat out an erratic pattern. Logan choked on his coffee as he tried to contain his laughter. Rikki shot him a glare before coming to David's side.

"Are you okay?" she asked, trying to conceal her own smile.

He narrowed his eyes at her failed attempt before looking back at me. "See what you do? Now my own mate is making fun of me."

"Suck it up," Dalton said, a playful smile forming on his face.

"Settle down, children," Ashlyn crooned, making her grand entrance.

"Good morning to you too, sunshine," I teased her.

She tossed me a nasty look over her shoulder as she made her way to the fridge like she owned the place. "You just started walking, Tor. Don't make me put you on bed rest again."

"Bring it on."

"Speaking of which," Logan said, speaking for the first time that morning and drawing my attention back to him. "Are you ready?"

"If I have to be," I grumbled.

I didn't want to fight, let alone fight him. He *was* my mate, and it was going to be extremely difficult to overcome the natural instinct to work *with* him instead of against him. As if he could hear the warring thoughts in my head, Logan came around the island counter to stand directly in front of me. He placed a finger under my chin and tilted my face until it forced me to meet those teal eyes of his.

"We don't have to. All you have to do is agree to stay and I'll retract the challenge," he murmured, just loud enough for me to hear.

The only thing standing between me and freedom was the man before me, and it was possibly one of the toughest decisions I had ever had to make. Having a mate was a complication I never thought I'd have to face. But now here I was, facing off against the one person who was supposed to mean everything to me.

How does someone cope with that?

"No. Let's go," I said, shaking my head to clear it. Right now, all I wanted was to get out of this town and away from this situation.

Logan's face immediately fell and hardened. "Alright," he said in a clipped voice before turning on his heel.

For a moment, I just stood there staring after him as he strode for the front door.

David came up beside me. "Tor, c'mon. You just recovered, but that doesn't mean you're up for a fight this quick. It really won't kill you to at least give him a chance to earn your acceptance."

My entire body bristled at the idea.

Accept the mate claim? What would the consequences be?

The idea of giving up my pack to stand beside Logan left a sour feeling in my stomach. What would happen to Ashlyn and Michael? Would he allow them to stay? Would they absorb David into Logan's pack automatically because of Rikki?

Question after question battered around inside my skull, and I could feel the onset of a headache.

"Torian?" Logan called, effectively quieting my mind. A scowl fitted onto my face as I started after him.

I was still cursing him under my breath when I ran smack into him in the hall.

"Could you watch where you're going?" I snapped, glaring up at him.

"Calm down, ma vie." His accompanying smile irritated me even more than I already was. He seemed to know it, too. When he reached out as if to embrace me, I wondered if he also knew I was considering removing his arm from his body.

"Let's just get this over with," I snarled, knocking into him as I shoved past.

"Follow me," he replied with a sigh. After giving me one last lingering look, he turned and opened the door, motioning for me to go out ahead of him.

After I marched out the door, it didn't take long before I realized I didn't know where I was going. Laughter erupted behind me, and when I turned around, I saw that the rest of our combined packs had made their way into the hall. Logan smirked before coming up to me and placing his hands on my shoulders.

"Don't even start," I warned when he opened his mouth.

His smile only grew. "Yes, ma'am," he said, laughter lacing his voice before he headed for the woods.

Having no choice but to follow him, I let a good twenty feet grow between us before I started moving. I could hear the rest of them traipsing along behind us, but I tried to ignore them. The only thing on my mind was how I was supposed to win this ridiculous fight. I was running over different strategies in my head when I bumped into Logan. He turned around with a bright smile on his face.

"Here we are," he said brightly, gesturing around the small clearing.

My gaze roamed the area, taking in everything I could use to my advantage. From the look of it, I was out of luck. The clearing was barren. The trees surrounding it may provide enough cover to dart in and out of if I played it right. Lips pursed, I let my attention fall on Logan, who was watching me through narrowed eyes.

"What're you doing?" he asked.

"Nothing," I replied with a shrug. He scowled, which just made me smile. "So, now what?"

"Shift."

"Fine."

Turning on my heel, I stalked off into the trees. Logan had the home field advantage here. He probably knew these woods like the back of his hand, which only spelled trouble for me. I couldn't afford to lose focus for even a second if I had any hope of winning this damn challenge.

When I was far enough away from everyone else, I slipped my shirt over my head. Reaching back to undo my bra, I paused as every hair on my body stood on end. My spine locked as the awareness of eyes on me crept over my skin. Raising my head, I slowly scanned the surrounding area. The trees were too skinny for anyone to hide behind, so I knew I was alone, save for the packs I had left a few yards back. The feeling ebbed, and I had no choice but to chalk it up to nerves.

Clenching my jaw, I allowed the uncomfortable feeling of bones shifting forms to run through me. It took less than a heartbeat and I was on all fours.

Shaking out my fur, I opened my eyes. Everything was so much clearer as I trotted back to where I had left Logan and the others. When I stepped out into the open, I was face to face with the hulking black wolf that lived under my mate's skin.

How had I forgotten how big he was?

He picked up on my unease. "*Scared, ma vie?*" he taunted, his voice echoing in my head. That stupid pet name held far too much affection for my liking.

"*Not even a little*," I lied. Bravado had always been one of my closest friends. I sunk into a crouch. Watching. Waiting.

I could sense my pack's nerves as Dalton stepped between us.

"This'll be a simple fight," he said, his voice echoing in the morning's quiet. "The first wolf to hold down his or her opponent for ten seconds will be declared the winner. Do we understand?" he asked, glancing between the two of us. We both nodded and Dalton backed up, leaving nothing but empty space between Logan and me. He crouched down, mimicking my position. "On three," Dalton called. "One. Two. *Three.*"

Logan and I growled in unison, but neither one of us made any move to attack.

I wanted to, but I was being held back by the bond. That cursed fucking thing. Even unaccepted, it was strong.

It was like trying to fight my way through a thick swamp, and my muscles just wouldn't cooperate. Instead of lunging for an attack, I circled Logan. His eyes watched every move I made, his own muscles tightly coiled and ready to spring. I saw his legs twitch, signaling he'd reclaimed control. He leapt toward me with a feral snarl and teeth bared.

I met him in the air.

The vampire didn't like this.

Not one little bit.

He knew the new pack on his land wouldn't end up boding well for him or his plans. He had enough trouble dealing with Logan's pack alone. Silently, he watched as the two wolves fought. He figured the new pack's Alpha had to be the white wolf, the small female he had seen trailing behind Logan earlier.

He didn't know her name, but there was something about her that had instantly captured his attention. He just couldn't quite put his finger on it.

The shifters had exchanged few words since he had followed them, so he didn't have a clue why the two were fighting. All he knew was that for being smaller than Logan, the white wolf was holding her own. Whenever Logan would lunge at her, she would be well out of harm's way before he was even back on the ground.

The sound of voices distracted him from the fight. "Do you think Torian's going to win?" the redhead from Logan's pack asked one of the newcomers.

"She won't go down easy," the boy said, reaching down and taking the redhead's hand in his own.

"I know, but what if she wins? Will you leave with her?" he heard the girl, Rikki, if he remembered correctly, ask the boy from the other pack.

"He's her mate, Rik. I'm not letting her leave here without giving him an honest chance."

The vampire smirked. *All good things to those who wait.*

So that's what the two were fighting about? The white wolf was Logan's mate, and she didn't want him?

A loud yelp drew his focus back to the two wolves. They were in stark contrast to each other, one black and one white, so it was easy to find them. Logan had Torian pinned beneath him, teeth at her throat. A deep growl rumbled in her chest before she ripped away from him, causing his bite to break skin.

The vampire winced as blood marred her otherwise pristine coat. She, however, seemed oblivious to it. Taking her eyes off Logan for the briefest of seconds, she glanced at the wound. He could almost hear her teeth grind together in frustration.

Her head raised to watch for Logan again. The black wolf was prowling close to the tree the vampire perched in.

As if she could sense him above them, her crystal eyes flicked up. When their eyes locked, one of the most feral snarls the vampire had heard erupted from her chest.

It was as good a time as any to make his presence known to the rest of them, so he dropped smoothly to the ground.

Nine pairs of eyes snapped to him and he couldn't keep the smile off his face.

Logan's teal eyes narrowed as he realized exactly who the vampire was.

Xander.

The black wolf stood straight before herding Torian into the trees and out of Xander's sight. The boy from Torian's pack that had been speaking earlier snarled at him.

"Vampire," he spat.

"Very good," Xander stated, searching the trees for the pair of Alpha's. He wasn't interested in any of the rest of them.

They emerged back into the clearing only seconds later, both in human form. The shirt that was covering Torian's frame was obviously Logan's, considering it all but swallowed her.

She looked incredible.

The thought took Xander by surprise. He hadn't felt genuine attraction for anyone, let alone a shifter, since-

"Xander," Logan said, cutting his thoughts short.

"Logan," the vampire greeted with a cordial smile.

The brunette attempted to make her way around Logan, but he held out an arm to stop her without taking his eyes off of Xander. "What are you doing here?" Logan questioned, eyes narrowing to slits at the vampire.

Xander shrugged. "Oh, you know. Just passing through before I caught sight of the recent additions." His eyes lingered over Torian, and he was rewarded with Logan's curled lip. Good. Then he could use her to get under Logan's skin.

"Stay away from her, Xander," Logan said, his voice deadly and practically dripping acid.

Xander grinned wide enough for his fangs to show. This was going to be too easy.

"I don't think I will," the vampire replied. "You see, I've figured out that she's important to you. Which means she could be extremely beneficial to me. Do you see where I'm going with this?"

"She has nothing to do with anything you're planning,"

"But she could play such a large part."

"I'm right here," Torian dead-panned, raising her hand. Logan tried to shush her, and she shot him a glare that would send lesser men running.

"It's a pleasure to meet you, Torian," Xander cooed, meeting her gaze.

"Wish I could say the same," she retorted, turning that glare on him. She made to move around Logan again, but he refused to let her even an inch closer to Xander. The vampire saw the exact moment her irritation reached its breaking point. She rounded on the Alpha that had been a thorn in Xander's side for years. "I can take care of myself," she hissed, batting his arm out of the way with enough force to make the other male wince. Xander began clapping. She rounded on him, eyes calculating as she took him in. "*Why* are you here?" she asked, mimicking Logan's earlier question.

"That's between your mate and I. So sorry," Xander told her, his voice layered with faux sweetness.

A low growl rumbled in her chest as her eyes flashed. She wanted to shift. He could feel it. From the look of unease filtering through the rest of the shifters, they could, too. They were each waiting on their Alpha's call. Logan's pack had been dealing with Xander for years. They knew his strength and knew that it would be suicide for at least some of them if they attacked.

Torian's pack knew no such thing and were just waiting for the order to strike.

Logan stepped to Torian's side, settling a calming hand on her shoulder. Xander wondered if she even realized that some of the tension in her stance fled at his touch.

"You came here for a reason," Logan said, fixing his stare on the meddlesome vampire. "Now spit it out."

Xander held his hands up in front of him before shoving them back into his pockets. "I just came to inform you we're done waiting on the sidelines. Year after year, our numbers dwindle as you and yours continue living on the land that is rightfully ours." Xander's teasing manner was gone, and his rage was bubbling to the surface. "There's an army rising against you, Logan. We're going to take back what you took, and we'll dispose of anyone who stands in our way." His gaze lingered on Torian before trailing to her pack. When he looked back at her, he could see the first sign of fear she had shown flickering over her face. Not for herself, but for her pack.

Logan growled, no doubt picking up on Xander's fixation with his mate. The sound rumbled deep in his chest as he nudged Torian away from him.

He lunged for Xander, shifting in midair.

Those teal eyes blazed with rage as he sailed past the vampire. Xander had been expecting his attack and moved out of the way with time to spare. He beckoned Logan to him, taunting him. The black wolf snarled as he advanced on the vampire again. Logan leapt, but Xander was through playing.

This time, when Logan flew at him, he stood his ground. He threw his fist forward when the wolf was within range.

A sickening crack sounded, and Logan's pained howl echoed off the trees. He slumped to the ground as his pack rushed to his side. That left Torian on the opposite side of the clearing, the vampire standing between her and her pack.

The realization hit Xander, and he turned to her with a satisfied smile, his fangs on full display. He could see the gears turning in her head as her crystalline eyes flicked between him and the two packs behind him. If she wanted to get to them, she had to get past him.

An idea struck Xander, and it was just too good of an opportunity to pass up.

In a blurred flash of movement, he was in front of Torian. She raised her gaze to meet his, and the urge to touch her was overwhelming. He fought it for only a moment before he gave in, cupping her jaw in his hand. The heat of her skin flooded through him, and there were equal parts of loathing and curiosity in her eyes as they narrowed on him.

He raised a finger to his lips, warning her to be quiet as he slipped behind her. When he refocused on the other side of the clearing, he had to stifle a laugh. It had been mere seconds since he had knocked Logan on his ass, and Torian's pack was advancing on them.

"Tell them to stop," he murmured, bringing his lips to the shell of her ear. "Or every single one of you is dead."

It was a bluff. He had come out alone today, but they didn't need to know that.

Torian held up her hand, and the three of hers stopped dead.

"What do you want with me?" she asked, her voice level even though he could feel the tremors running through her.

"To torture Logan," he said, locking eyes with the wolf in question. Logan hadn't shifted back yet, and he was struggling to get himself upright. "This'll only hurt a little, darling," he warned.

And it was the only one he gave before he sank his fangs deep into Torian's throat.

Chapter Eight

THE PAIN TOOK A second to register.

His fangs sank deep, and I gritted my teeth against the dull throb. I had been bitten before. Many times.

But Xander began to feed, and that's when I screamed.

He may as well have been dragging my very soul out of those two punctures. My blood turned to acid, burning against my veins as it left me. I tried to fight, to *move*, but I couldn't. The venom that coated a vampire's fangs was vicious, and with his fangs still seated in my throat, that venom was having plenty of time to wreak havoc on my system. It was like it had disconnected my muscles from my brain.

But that earsplitting cry caught the attention of everyone else. My pack disregarded my earlier order and sprinted for me.

I could feel Xander's grin against my throat as he removed his fangs. Just before David reached us, the vampire launched us into the trees.

He maneuvered through the woods with unnatural grace. I had rarely come in contact with an older vampire, and with a stroke of genuine fear, I realized how little I truly knew about them. Newborns were a dime a dozen, but I was quickly understanding I was at a disadvantage against the predator holding me.

In less time than I could keep track of, we were inside a cabin. Xander laid me down on a cot with care. I had about two heartbeats to take in the sparsely decorated room before he climbed back on top of me. A deep growl bubbled up my throat as his eyes met mine.

They were the color of quicksilver, and they flashed with something like regret as he bent back to my neck. His mouth brushed over my skin with a featherlight touch, and he kissed the puncture wound before running his cool tongue across it.

The venom was still working through my system, and I wasn't sure how much blood he had taken, but I felt useless. Weak.

"What did you just do?" I croaked. My vocal chords felt like sandpaper rubbing together.

"Healed you. You're welcome," he replied, his voice calm and collected.

"I'm going to kill you for this," I threatened, though it was pathetic even to my own ears.

"You can try," he murmured, leaning in so that his nose brushed mine.

"Back off."

"I don't think I will." He settled himself next to my hip, and I glared at him. One corner of his lip tilted up as he placed his hand across my throat. My spine locked up, but he didn't apply any pressure. Vampires ran a few degrees colder than a normal human, so his cool skin felt like a balm against the inflamed wound. I fought not to sigh at the relief that touch brought.

"What do you want from me?' I asked, keeping my voice low.

"Right now, I just want you to regain some of your strength so I can return you to Logan."

"So you're not going to kill me?"

"Not today."

There was history there, and I needed to know what it was. But I was in no position to push this vampire for answers. And I had no idea how long it would take for my strength to return. So for the time being, I had to take him at his word.

I took a moment to take in the room. It was barren of any personal touches. But what was I expecting? There was a small kitchenette on the far side, and I could see a door that I was assuming led to a bathroom. When I swung my attention back to Xander, he was watching me.

Two predators, sizing each other up to see which one of them would end up prey.

I bared my teeth.

He chuckled, and the sound was obnoxiously warm and inviting. "Simmer down," he said, removing his hand. "You're safe."

Biting back my retort, I just rolled my eyes. Slowly but surely, I could feel my strength returning. And gods above knew I wasn't about to let him *return* me like some errant child. I'd get myself back to the pack house.

Xander walked away from me, headed toward the fridge, and I made a break for it. My world tilted on its axis as I whipped into a sitting position. Taking a deep breath, I fought against the vertigo and dashed for the door we had initially come through.

I had already shifted, shredding Logan's t-shirt, before the door banged against the wall.

Taking a guess at which direction the house was, I took off at a stumbling sprint. It didn't take long for me to realize I was not in any condition to be running. My vision was spotting, and I tripped more than once. In this condition, there was no way I was making it back in once piece if I didn't rest.

Coming to a halt, I closed my eyes and focused on the surrounding sounds. My ears twitched as I tried to pick up any sound of pursuit. Finding none, I opened my eyes and spied a wide oak tree. I made my way over to it and slumped down against it. I knew in my heart that if I fell asleep, the chances of Xander catching back up to me were high. But between the exertion of the shift, the run, the venom, and the blood loss, I was fighting to stay conscious.

I had to have dozed off for a bit, because the next thing I knew, there were a pair of black boots mere inches from my nose. Lifting my head to see him, I took in the glare Xander was aiming at me. But that glare dissolved into a look of worry as I tried to stand, only to crumple right back down into a useless heap of white fur.

He crouched in front of me, and I growled. He smiled, but just shushed me as he moved. His hand ghosted over my head as he took up a vigil at my side.

"You can rest, Torian," he said, his lilting voice barely carrying. "I'll get you home."

I let out an indignant snort and continued to fight to stay awake, but it was a losing battle. Huffing, I laid my head on my paws and allowed my eyes to flutter closed. I was exhausted, and

I couldn't hold back the shift to human form. The spring air nipped at the newly exposed skin, and it barely registered that Xander pulled me into him. Something soft slipped around me, warding off the chill that wanted to set in.

I needed to pry for information, but I lost the fight with consciousness before I could even open my mouth.

The vase crashed against the wall, filling the room with the sound of shattering glass.

Logan's chest was heaving as he watched the shards cascade to the floor. He didn't have a clue where Xander had taken Torian or what he was doing to her, and it was killing him. He should have been able to protect her.

"We'll find her, Logan," Brooke soothed, coming up and placing a gentle hand on his shoulder. Ever the voice of reason in Logan's pack.

"I don't see why we can't just go after them now," David said, just as on edge as Logan.

"Because Xander is hundreds of years old," Brooke told him, turning to meet the Beta's stare. "We don't know the full extent of his power, and we don't know what he'll do to Torian if we go in half cocked. We need to know where they are, and we need a plan."

David blew out a heavy sigh, but nodded. Rikki moved to stand by him, taking his hand firmly in hers. She knew he was blaming himself for what had happened. Knew that Logan was too. But David was Torian's Beta, her right hand. She knew he was thinking he had failed to protect Torian.

And Rikki would bet he'd lay down his life for his Alpha, just like they all would for Logan.

"We'll bring her back safe and sound," she told him, brushing his chestnut hair out of his eyes.

Logan watched the pair and could barely stand it. The pang of jealousy echoed through him, because that ease was what he had always envisioned when he pictured finding his mate. He sat on the couch, placing his head in his hands as he wracked his brain. He didn't even know where to begin to look for Xander. Ever since they had run him out of his mansion in the foothills, they hadn't heard a peep from the meddlesome vampire.

Of all times, now was when he decided to come back?

To declare war?

Hadn't he taken enough from Logan already?

He could feel the headache developing, but he had to focus. Dalton came up to him, clapping him on the shoulder as a somber look settled onto the younger shifter's face.

"What are our orders?" he asked.

"We need a plan to find them," Logan said, wincing as he stood. His ribs protested every move he made, and he was sure some of them had fractured, if not broken. But until he had Torian back, he didn't have to time to let himself heal.

"We'll do whatever you need us to," Ashlyn said, coming forward. He almost smiled, understanding that her civility was nothing more than an indicator of how badly she wanted Torian back.

Logan's eyes met David's, and it was as if there was a silent communication between the two.

Whatever it takes.

Logan was just about to split the packs up into search parties when a knock sounded at the door.

A growl built in Logan's chest as he sensed who it was, but it instantly changed to relief as he detected another presence as well.

Torian's.

He could feel her heartbeat as if it were an extension of his own, and he all but ran for the front door. He didn't bother offering the others an explanation. They'd be right behind him.

Logan wrenched the door open to find Xander standing there, holding Torian's limp and sleeping form in his arms. "Evening, Logan," the vampire greeted, silver eyes glittering with malice.

Logan wanted nothing more than to punch that self-satisfied smirk right off Xander's face, but he didn't dare as long as he still had Torian in his grasp.

"Give her to me," he said between gritted teeth, barely leashing his anger. He could feel everyone else gathering around the door, and he knew David was the one directly behind him.

"On one condition," Xander said, cradling Torian closer to him, which only caused a feral snarl to rip free of Logan's chest. The vampire just chuckled. "None of you attack me or try to come after me. Once I hand her over, I'm free and clear to walk away."

"Are you kidding me?" David seethed. "I should rip you limb from limb right here."

"Do we have a deal?" Xander asked, acting as if David hadn't even spoken.

"Yes," Ashlyn said, beating Logan to the punch. She moved to stand directly beside him and looked Xander dead in the eye. "Just give her back and we won't follow."

"Good girl," Xander purred, causing Ashlyn to curl her lip at him. Sighing, he gazed down at Torian in a way that made Logan's stomach churn. It was the same way he used to look at-

"Xander," Logan snapped, cutting his own thoughts short. "My mate, if you please." Xander brushed a strand of hair out of her face before gently placing her into Logan's arms. Before anyone could blink, he was gone.

"I'll kill him," Ashlyn and David said simultaneously as Logan kicked the door shut behind him.

"You're in line behind me," he told them, moving toward his bedroom. Torian's breathing was low and even, but he couldn't fathom why she hadn't woken up during the altercation at the door. He was worried, and he needed time to reassure himself she was okay.

He laid her on the bed, noting the shirt that was swallowing her. Xander's. That he had seen her in that state of vulnerability caused Logan's blood to heat, but he took a deep breath. She had to have shifted.

She had fought.

But what had Xander done that had caused her to be in this state? Logan's breaths were coming quicker, his fists clenching and unclenching as he tried to wrestle his emotions under control. He barely registered the sound of the door opening behind him.

"Breathe," Brooke ordered, coming to his side. And he did, focusing on inhaling and exhaling until the tremors had stopped . As he worked to calm himself, Brooke pressed two fingers against Torian's pulse. He could hear Torian's steady heartbeat, but he knew Brooke had an affinity for healing. She'd probably be the next pack doctor if she stayed on the track she was.

"Thank you," he murmured, never letting his eyes stray from Torian's sleeping form.

"She's alive, Logan. Focus on that. Give her time to heal. A fight with you, followed by a vampire attack, would drain even the strongest of shifters. And while she is strong, she's not invincible."

"When do you think she'll wake up?" he asked. He knew she was right, but he was still reluctant to leave the room.

Brooke shrugged before turning him away from Torian. She ignored his irritated growl and steered him out of the room. "I don't have a clue, but let her be for now."

He let out a resigned sigh and shrugged her off before making his way into the kitchen. He braced himself against the island counter.

How could he have been so careless?

He was about to go on berating himself before he heard the clearing of a throat behind him. He turned and only felt mild surprise when he saw Ashlyn leaning against the wall.

"You really care about her, don't you?" she asked, not really looking at him, more like she was looking through him.

"You're mated, you know what it's like. I'd do anything for her."

She nodded. "You're right. Michael and I found each other because of Tor. We owe our relationship to her. So it's time I repay that debt." She locked eyes with him, and he knew he was looking at Torian's third in command, the one who would die for her Alpha. No questions asked. "It's time she realized she can't run on her own forever. As long as you are the man she needs you to be, Michael and I will try to convince her to stay."

"That's a promise I can make."

A small smile tugged at the edges of her mouth. "You had better," she muttered before turning on her heel and leaving him alone once again.

Having all of Torian's pack on his side made him feel significantly better about winning her over. He knew she wouldn't leave them behind. So if they were *all* set on staying, then she would too.

He let loose a sigh of relief before slipping back to his bedroom. In the state she was in, he couldn't stand to be away from her for any extended period. He was sure the unaccepted bond didn't help matters, but he was too tired to question it.

Prying my eyes open, I had to blink a few times to force Logan's ceiling into focus. There was a body radiating heat into mine, and I didn't have to turn to know who it belonged to. Easing myself into a sitting position, I scooted to the edge of the bed before standing.

Glancing over my shoulder, I smiled at the way Logan's hair fell over his forehead. There was a crease of worry between his brows, and I knew it was for me. Without considering what I was doing, I leaned forward to brush the hair from his face. I trailed my fingertips over his browbone, and the lines smoothed out beneath my touch.

Sighing, I turned and headed for the bathroom. The door creaked as I opened it, and I paused, turning to check on Logan. His chest still rose and fell evenly. He hadn't even stirred. I slipped into the bathroom and shut the door behind me.

Drawing in a deep, steadying breath, I faced myself in the mirror.

My eyes were puffy and bloodshot, and there was a cut running the full length of my cheekbone. Gods knew when that had happened. But other than that, I seemed to be okay. I knew it could have been so much worse.

The clothes caught my attention. Xander's clothes.

My heart started pounding as I moved closer to the mirror. There was only one thing left to check, and I was dreading it. My hands were trembling as I moved my hair off my right shoulder, revealing where Xander had bitten me.

I blinked.

In place of the wound I was expecting to see, there was a six-point star. It looked like a brand, the skin shiny, raised, and a few shades lighter than the skin surrounding it. Like scar tissue.

Shaking my head, I let my hair fall like a curtain over the star. My feet moved backwards until my back met the door. Letting out a series of shallow pants, I slid down it until I was sitting on the floor.

That son of a bitch had *marked* me.

Chapter Nine

T HE CASCADE OF WARM water was welcoming when I finally slipped under it. An audible sigh escaped my mouth as the scalding water massaged my aching muscles. I stood under the water for the longest time. It took everything in me not to scrub my skin raw to get the feeling of Xander's cool touch off me, but the heat cleared my head.

The water ran cold way before I was ready, but I stepped out anyway. As I was wrapping a towel around myself, I snuck a glance at the discarded shirt on the floor. The first chance I got, I was burning it.

It took a few minutes of rummaging around in the closet, but I finally found a pair of sweats and a t-shirt from Logan's things that looked like they would at least somewhat fit. I had to roll the waistline of the sweats a few times, but they'd do. After ensuring they wouldn't fall back down, I crept back into the bedroom.

A glance at the clock had me doing a double take. It was two in the morning. How had that even happened? Letting out a soft sigh, I crawled in next to Logan, putting my back to him. My mind wandered as I laid there.

How had I gotten into this? The mate claim was hard enough to handle. But now I had to deal with a vampire too? A potential war?

Thinking about it all had me stifling a groan. Especially about that damn mate claim. Even as I tried to deny it, I could feel it growing with every moment Logan and I spent with each other. If I wasn't careful, it was going to consume me completely. It was just the way the magic worked. Once the two mates meet, the claim is made. It's up to both sides to accept it before the bond solidifies, tying them together for eternity.

Logan had already accepted it on his end. That much was obvious. And the longer we were in each other's orbit, the harder it would be for me to keep rejecting it. It would keep growing strength, burrowing farther into my very soul.

Which was why I wanted to get out of here. The sooner the better.

I wished I just knew what the right decision was. Maybe I *wasn't* doing the right thing in rejecting him, but then again, did I want to take that risk? Turning to face him, I allowed myself to trace the worry lines on his forehead with the tips of my fingers. They smoothed out almost instantly, and Logan stirred. His hand lifted to grasp mine, and then his eyes fluttered open.

"Ma vie," he breathed, wrapping his arms around my waist before crushing me against him. "You're awake."

I laughed. "Of course I am."

"Are you okay?" he asked, pulling back and holding me at arm's length.

"I've been worse." And I wasn't lying.

"Are you sure?" His eyes narrowed before scanning over me.

"Were you worried about me?" I teased, trying to make light of the whole situation.

"Are you kidding me? Of course, I was worried about you. You were out for two days."

There was a beat of silence, and I felt the color drain from my face.

"Two days?"

"What did he *do,* Torian?" He cupped my cheek in his palm, and even though his voice and touch were gentle, I could almost feel the maelstrom of emotions thrashing inside him.

He needed to know.

Sitting up, I pulled him with me before sweeping my hair off my shoulder. "I don't exactly know how this stuff works, but..."

"He marked you?" he ground out between clenched teeth, tracing his fingers lightly across the star that was now branded into my neck.

Nodding, I let my hair fall back to cover it. "Do you know what it means?"

"I'm sure you know that vampires just get more powerful with age?" His eyebrow quirked with his question, and I nodded. "Some of that is physical strength, some of it mental, and for some, it's magic. Xander's mark allows him access to the bearer's dreams."

"Is there a way to remove it?" Magic was such a bitch sometimes.

He gave a curt nod. "If he doesn't willingly remove it, one of you has to die."

A growl built in my throat. "How do you know so much about him?" I asked. When I had to strike out on my own, I cut my education into the magic of our world short. I had very little knowledge of anything outside of lupine shifters, and even that was only the basics.

Something I was learning I needed to remedy.

"He's been here for hundreds of years. Our pack has kept records of him and any other vampires that frequent the area. At least with as much information as we can truly gather."

It was my turn to narrow my eyes. He was hiding something.

But considering all I wasn't divulging, maybe I just needed to let it go.

"You'll have to share that with me at some point," I said.

"Just let me know when." He pulled me into him, tucking my head under his chin. "I am sorry I wasn't able to protect you."

"Logan," I murmured, allowing myself to relax into him. I think we both needed the support. "You don't need to apologize. I'm a big girl. I can take care of myself. And it wasn't your fault." He grunted, the closest I was guessing I would get to acceptance. "But you can tell me what the hell he's talking about with this war."

He blew out a breath before laying down, pulling me with him. "It's a long story," he warned. "When our pack first settled here, probably three centuries ago at this point, the area was infested with vampires. But the pack fell in love with the land, so we were willing to coexist with them." He chuckled to himself, but it was devoid of humor. "They weren't having it. It started a war. A long and bloody war. But we did eventually win. The few survivors surrendered, and our generations have lived here ever since.

"But Xander, he's never let it go. He was in the original war, and he comes back every few years to stir up trouble. Normally it's just scare tactics, a bad injury for one of us here and there, but never anything drastic. Until I came to power. I don't know why *now*, but he's become more than a nuisance. None of the pack runs solo anymore. It's why we were all in a group that first day you ran into us."

He sighed before he continued, "But with what he said the other day, he's not working alone anymore. He must have gotten in contact with one of the other survivors. But it's going to come to another war. I just know it."

The information swirled in my head as I tried to process. They had kept this territory free of vampires for over three hundred years? That was a feat to be admired, and a newfound admiration for the male at my side began to set in.

"So, what are we going to do?" I asked.

A smile twitched at the corners of his mouth. "We?" he parroted.

I swatted his chest. "Shut up. We both know I was about to lose our fight. Not to mention my shiny new mark, that means I'm tied to the vampire in question. I'm in this, whether I like it or not." He opened his mouth, pain swimming in those teal eyes. "Don't you dare apologize again."

"Fine," he murmured, brushing a strand of hair out of my face. "But you have to give this a fair shot. Staying isn't the whole of the agreement."

Scowling, I nodded. His eyes searched mine in the dim light, and I raised my brows at him. He grinned, and it was the only warning I got.

His lips were on mine, and a fire spread through my body so fiercely it took everything in me not to moan into his mouth. Instead, I wrapped my arms around his neck and pulled him closer. It was instinct. The kiss was soft and sweet, but Logan pulled away before it could escalate any further. Our gazes held, and our chests pressed together with every panting breath we took.

"What was that for?" I asked.

"I've been waiting to do that since I laid eyes on you," he said, eyes sparkling. "But we'll take things slow. I want this, but I want you to want it too."

He laid back down and pulled my back flush against his chest. He enveloped me in his comforting warmth, a gentle reminder of a peacefulness I had almost forgotten existed.

Logan was worried about her.

What if Xander invaded her mind while she slept? The thought caused a growl to rumble in his chest, and he pulled her closer to him. She was so peaceful. He hoped he was wrong.

But he knew from experience that once Xander fixated on someone, it was near impossible to derail the vampire's plans. He moved Torian's hair from the brand, tracing it. It wasn't the first time he'd seen it, but it physically pained him to see it blaring so starkly against the rest of Torian's porcelain skin.

His mind wandered, finally settling on thoughts of her pack. He hoped that having her in the house had settled them a bit, because all three had been beside themselves since Xander took her. He had seen the glances exchanged between David and Ashlyn. Torian's second and third, the two who held themselves accountable to keeping her safe. Not that they all wouldn't, but he didn't doubt that those two would have sacrificed anything to get her back.

But she *was* back, and she was safe. Relatively unscathed, save for the brand Xander had left behind.

Relieved didn't even come close to covering how Logan had felt the moment he opened his eyes to meet hers for the first time in two days.

Torian let out a whimper, pulling him from his thoughts. As she began to toss and turn, he knew his fears hadn't been in vain.

Xander had made himself known in her dreams.

Chapter Ten

I WAS BACK IN that damn cabin.

"Hello again, darling," Xander's voice carried to me, and I scowled into the darkness.

Stifling a growl, I raised into a sitting position. Xander wasn't hard to locate, leaning against the wall at the foot of the bed. His posture was languid, comfortable. Alarm bells pealed in the back of my mind, but I forced my voice to come out even when I asked, "What do you want?"

"I just wanted to check on you," he said, shrugging as he pushed off the wall. "You've been out for a while."

"Blood loss, exhaustion, and magic don't mix well for me, apparently."

He laughed lightly, sitting down at the very edge of the bed. My brows furrowed. He was keeping his distance.

Interesting.

"How are you feeling?" he asked, quicksilver eyes running over me as if he could assess the damage himself.

"I'm fine." His brows raised, and I felt a push against my mind that had my hackles raising. "What was that?"

"Habit, sorry," he shot me a grin, not an ounce of remorse on his face.

"What did you mean by I've been out for a while?"

His eyes shot to my neck, and the mark felt like it heated under his attention. He inclined his head toward it. "That allows me to know when you're asleep, so that I can make this happen." He gestured to the surrounding cabin. "So I know you've been asleep since I dropped you off."

"Couldn't have given me more time to recover?"

He grinned, fangs flashing. "I was worried."

"Yeah, okay," I replied, snorting.

Our eyes clashed and held, both of us sizing the other up. I didn't know what he wanted with me, but I knew he was powerful. Probably the most powerful vampire I had ever encountered. I had to tread carefully

Those quicksilver eyes softened, and he leaned against the footboard behind him. "I was. I took more blood than I intended, and the mark was a split second decision that is also draining."

"Why me?"

"Because it gives me something over Logan," he said, shrugging.

"You expect me to believe that's it?"

"No."

"Can I go back now?"

A small smile formed before he nodded, and those silver eyes faded away with the rest of the cabin.

When my eyes opened and refocused, I sat bolt upright in bed. It was almost like I could still feel Xander prowling around the edge of my subconscious, and I had to shake myself to banish the feeling.

"Ma vie?" Logan's voice was quiet as he sat up next to me.

"I'm fine."

"What happened?"

Blowing out a breath, I turned to face him. His teal eyes seemed to glow in the pre-dawn light, and I allowed myself to admit that the sight of him had already become a point of comfort for me.

Just not out loud. Damn shifter hormone.

"Nothing," I reassured him. He still looked skeptical. "He just said he had been worried. Apparently, he can sense when I'm asleep, thanks to the mark. So he knew I was out the whole time."

Something unreadable flashed across Logan's face before he closed his eyes. He breathed deeply for a moment before pulling me into him.

"I'm going to kill him," he muttered, burying his face in the crook of my neck.

"Only if you let me help."

When he pulled back, there was a smile on his face. "Deal."

We settled back into the covers, and I let myself sink into his warmth as I laid my head on his chest. He trailed his fingers up and down my arm, leaving goosebumps in his wake.

Slowly, light filled the room, but neither of us made a move to get up. I had been hoping I'd be able to fall back asleep, but I didn't see it happening anytime soon.

"I have news," Logan said once the sun had fully risen.

"What's that?"

"My parents should return home today."

I felt like someone had dumped ice straight down my spine. Something like fear swirled in my gut, and I raised up on my elbow to meet Logan's gaze.

"And?" I asked, brows quirked.

"You should meet them."

"And why would I do that?"

"Because you're staying in their home, for starters." At my glare, he just grinned. "You're my mate, Torian. They'll want to meet you."

"Not if you don't tell them."

"How else am I supposed to explain a pack of nomads staying with us?"

He had a point.

"Fine," I ground out. "But I'm not pretending, Logan."

"I would never ask you to," he replied, leaning up to kiss my forehead. "They should be in around lunchtime. Let's go prep the others."

My eyes rolled of their own accord as I shoved past him and made my way toward the kitchen. Logan trailed behind, brushing his hand over mine when I stopped at the island to take a seat. He started a pot of coffee, and I drummed my fingers against the granite countertop.

How was I supposed to maneuver this? I *had* told Logan I would give this a shot, but I didn't want it to stick. I still wanted to leave. Logan's pack, his family, were territorial wolves. I was lucky none of them had figured out the truth yet. But his *parents?* They could know who I was. They might know the truth the minute I introduced myself, and then what was I supposed to do?

Logan set a steaming cup of coffee on the counter in front of me and placed a finger under my chin when I failed to look up. He tilted my face until our eyes met.

"They're going to love you," he said, picking up on my anxiety. I wasn't about to tell him he had the reasoning behind it wrong.

"If you say so," I murmured. He used the pad of his thumb to brush against my bottom lip as he released me. His eyes studied me for a moment, but as the rest of the house woke up around us, he must have decided to let it go.

For now.

))))))OCCCCC

"Please don't," the man whimpered in her arms.

She withdrew her bleeding wrist from his mouth and rolled her eyes.

"Shut up," she said before snapping his neck. With her venom and her blood in his system, he'd wake up a vampire within hours.

"Raven, you have got to stop killing so many from the same town," a masculine voice called from the darkness behind her.

She spun around and glared at Xander as he materialized out of the shadows. "You want an army? Don't tell me how to build it." She threw the corpse at his feet. "Your newest edition," she sneered, turning on her heel to walk away.

"Raven."

His voice stopped her in her tracks, as it always had. She didn't bother turning around as she hissed, "What?"

He circled her, his eyes calculating as they took her in. She tried to ignore it, the way she wanted to preen under his attention. He had always been her superior, a commander in the war when she had been nothing more than a soldier. And with him being her senior by over a century, she always bowed to him in the end.

No matter how much she hated it.

He finally came to a stop in front of her, flashing her favorite smirk. "Aren't you happy to see me?"

"Not particularly."

She knew the lecture he was about to spout off, and she didn't want to hear it. She continued into the woods, heading toward the cabin he had claimed not too long ago.

He fell into step beside her, and they walked in silence. She tried to focus on her next steps with gaining new vampires. Whether she should continue to make newborns to use as fodder in the oncoming war with the shifters, or if she should spread out. See if she could find any of the other survivors of the first war.

"They're not interested," Xander said, answering her thoughts out loud. "I went through damn near all of them before I found you."

"Glad to know I was a last resort," she muttered, kicking at a loose stone in her path. "And stay out of my head."

"Don't think so loud."

She glared at him, furious that he could just waltz through her thoughts whenever he pleased. His power had its limits, but he had free rein when he was this close to her. Xander's telepathy had morphed over the years into his ability to mark, which gave him much more control over the bearer. She was lucky to have never received one.

She knew he was aware of her power of persuasion. Similar to Xander's ability, she could influence people, but she couldn't get inside their head. Only give them nudges in the direction she wanted. It wasn't nearly as strong as Xander's power, but it was one reason they had always gotten along. They understood one another.

But he was pushing her buttons today.

"What did you find out about the pack?" she asked, trying to steer the conversation away from her.

"Logan found his mate."

Raven drew up short, her midnight hair whipping around her with the sudden stop. "Who?"

"A nomad."

"Was she alone?"

"Small pack. Just four total."

That was good. They could deal with four. Logan joining with another full pack would've thrown a nasty wrench into their plans.

"I marked her."

Raven blinked. Once. Twice. Slowly, she turned until she was facing the other vampire.

What *was* it with him and the shifters?

"That was stupid," she stated.

"I'm aware."

"Then *why* did you do it?"

He shrugged and had the good sense to look sheepish. He rubbed the back of his neck as he cast his gaze skyward. "It was just something to fuck with Logan at first."

"And now?"

"She reminds me of her."

Oh, for *fuck's* sake.

The growl that built in her chest couldn't be helped.

"You're playing with fire, Xander," she warned. "Don't come crying to me when it burns you to ash."

He gave her a crooked little smile that made her see red. Shaking her head at him, she changed course. She wouldn't be returning to the cabin with him tonight.

She had an army to build him, after all.

Chapter Eleven

"Stop fidgeting," Rikki ordered, brandishing the brush at me through the mirror.

"Sorry," I muttered, pursing my lips. "But I can get myself ready, you know."

"She enjoys doing this," Brooke called from where she was lying across the bed, watching us with a small grin on her face. "Don't take it away from her."

My eyes rolled, but I kept my mouth shut as the redhead continued to brush through my hair. Whatever she had done with it, the dark brown strands shone. Ashlyn handed me a tube of mascara and I continued to apply a little makeup while Rikki finished up.

Meeting his parents. What a joke. Logan had to be insane.

Maybe that was why we had ended up mated.

"You're going to be fine, Tor," Ashlyn said, giving me a small smile.

My eyes narrowed at her. She had been more and more accepting of Logan lately, and it was giving me the creeps.

"Since we're going for a stellar first impression here," Brooke started, making her way over to Rikki's closet. "I'm going to find you something to wear."

Trying not to roll my eyes, I swiped on a little lipstick and called it good. Rikki dropped the last curl into place only a second later, and I spun on the vanity stool to await Brooke's return.

Why did I even care what they thought of me? I was going to break their son's heart in the end, anyway.

Before my thoughts could spiral too far down that road, Brooke emerged with a bundle of clothes in her arms. She just laughed when I arched my brows at her.

"Jeans or a dress?"

"Jeans, please."

She placed a few things back into the closet before handing me the jeans I asked for and a soft black sweater. It wasn't over the top, but decidedly nicer than the old t-shirt of Logan's I currently had on. Slipping into the new clothes, I almost missed Rikki setting a pair of black boots out for me as well.

Thank the gods Rikki and I were roughly the same size. Ashlyn suspiciously had new clothes, but I hadn't had the chance to grill her about them yet.

"You ready?" Rikki asked, grinning as she gave me a quick once over.

"As I'll ever be."

She rolled her hazel eyes at me before grabbing my arm and towing me toward the door. Brooke and Ashlyn laughed, trailing behind us as we headed for the living room. I fought against the urge to dig my heels in, because what would be the point? The fact was we were staying in these people's home, and I probably should meet them.

Rikki all but shoved me into the living room, and I didn't even have a chance to glare at her before Logan spotted me.

Why did he have to look so good?

Seeing him in something other than a t-shirt was jarring. Apparently, he had also dressed up in celebration of his parent's return. His navy blue button down hugged his shoulders, and he had his sleeves rolled back to expose his forearms. I had to stop my mouth from watering at the picture he painted. His hair wasn't as wild as usual, but the same couldn't be said for his eyes.

Those teal orbs ran over me with reverence, and it made my heart speed up when they met mine again.

He was in front of me too soon. I hadn't even realized he'd moved. He stopped less than a foot away from me, flexing his hands by his side like he was trying to stop himself from reaching for me.

Which was stupid. If either of us took too deep of a breath, our chests would brush.

"You look beautiful," he said, voice rough.

"You're not too bad yourself."

He leaned in, and even though my mind was screaming at me to move, I couldn't.

His lips were a hairsbreadth away from mine, and his eyes locked on mine again, seeking permission.

"We're home!" a masculine voice boomed, shattering the moment.

Taking a deep breath, I tried to steady myself as the packs fell in behind Logan and me. Logan grinned before snagging my waist and pulling me closer to him. I glanced at him out of the corner of my eye before clasping my hands behind my back to keep them from shaking. If he could feel the slight tremor running through me, he didn't comment. But he slipped his hand in between mine, offering comfort without it being obvious.

"Kids?" the same voice from earlier called.

"Logan? Dalton?" a much more feminine voice added.

"In here!" the brothers chorused.

"Now what's with all the…" the man that could only be Logan's father trailed off as he saw the four newest additions in his living room. He had the same eyes as Dalton, as well as the same angular features and hair color the brothers shared. My gaze flicked to the woman. She was probably a few inches taller than me, and her hair was a deep mahogany color that flowed over her shoulders in soft curls. But it was her eyes that caught my attention. They were the same enchanting shade of teal as the man that stood at my side.

"Welcome home," Logan said, drawing their attention to us.

My spine straightened as they scanned from head to toe. Logan squeezed my hand, and some of the tension dropped from my shoulders. But I kept my chin high, meeting their gazes head on.

"And who are they?" his father asked, sweeping the rest of us with a keen eye. The man before me may not be the Alpha anymore, but it was easy to see that he had been.

"This is Torian, my mate, and her friends."

Friends. I almost rolled my eyes. Logan was trying to get a rise out of me. To what end, I didn't know. But he knew damn well there was a big distinction between *friends* and *pack* when it came to our kind.

Logan's father must have caught the dirty look I shot his son, because his mouth quirked up at the corners. "Did you have something to add to that?"

"They're my pack," I said, fighting not to elbow Logan in the gut when I felt him shaking with barely contained laughter.

"Nomads?" he asked. I nodded in response, knowing what was coming next. His gaze flicked to Michael, and then back to me. "And your Alpha is?"

"Me," I stated, putting as much force into that single word as I could. I knew it wasn't common for a female shifter to take the place as Alpha, but it wasn't unheard of. But every time, I still felt the need to make it crystal clear.

Logan's father blinked in surprise, but his wife let out a tinkling laugh as she patted his chest. She looked at me, eyes dancing with mirth as she grinned. "Don't mind him," she said, crossing the distance between us all and holding her hand out to me. "I'm Kenna Grey."

"Torian," I said, even though Logan had already introduced me. I purposefully left out my last name, just as I always did. The Pierce pace had a wide reach in the shifter world, and I wanted no association with them.

Her brows quirked up, but she didn't question it. She glanced over her shoulder at her husband, and he made his way over as well. "Nicholas Grey," he said, smiling now. "Nick is fine."

He shook my hand, and I finished the introductions of my pack. Nicholas's eyes snagged on Rikki's hand that was securely wrapped in David's, and his eyes crinkled at the corners as he grinned.

Rikki chucked one of the throw pillows off the couch at him before he could even speak. "Shut up, Nick," she said, her face turning the same shade as her hair.

"So you found your mate too, Red?"

"Sure did." The smile on her face was infectious, and I couldn't help but grin as she and David locked eyes. I knew exactly how happy they were for Rikki, because I was over the moon for David.

"Seems your turning up has done a lot of good," Kenna commented.

"I guess so," I said.

It didn't take long for everyone to disperse. The couples headed off in their separate directions, and Dalton made an excuse that he was going to head off with his friends. Which left Logan and me alone in the living room.

"That wasn't so bad, was it?" he asked.

"Your little set-up was cute."

"Caught that, did you?"

"Do you just enjoy seeing me riled?"

"Immensely." He spun me to face him, a kilowatt smile stretching across his face. His eyes flicked to my lips, and I didn't even bother with hesitating. Pushing up onto my tiptoes, I finished what we had started before we were interrupted.

Chapter
Twelve

X ANDER COCKED HIS HEAD to the side as he gazed through the window.

He hadn't intended to be a peeping Tom today, but he had known that Logan's parents were supposed to return home and had wanted a front-row seat when they did.

For someone who didn't want a mate, Torian was enveloped in Logan like he was the only thing that existed.

He hummed softly to himself as he turned and made his way toward the cabin he was starting to call home. He made it all the way to the threshold before he scented her.

Raven.

She was sitting on the cot, one leg propped up as she read one of his books, the other leg swinging next to the corpse on the ground.

He was still debating if recruiting her had been a mistake. Raven had always been a loose cannon, even during the first war. But he had always seen promise in her. And with her ability, she was a valuable asset in what he was trying to do.

But she was testing his patience.

"Really?" he asked, shutting the door behind him a little louder than necessary.

She barely raised her eyes from the page. "You wanted this army quick," she reminded him, dog-earring the page before setting the book down beside her. As always, she had dressed for stealth in head to toe black. Which, considering she was basically out murdering humans, was probably a good idea. She grinned at him, fangs flashing as she gestured to the body. "So, try not to tell me how to do my job."

He sighed, rolling his eyes skyward before discarding his jacket onto the back of one of the kitchen chairs. He braced his hands against it before he met Raven's icy blue stare.

"Do you have a plan for training them yet?" he asked, deciding not to pick that exact fight with her right now. If anyone was capable of keeping the newborns in check, it was the two of them. And Raven had learned everything she knew about combat and war from him, so she was one of few he could trust to delegate the task to.

"I was hoping to pick your brain on that," she said, standing and stretching her arms above her head. "We can't keep them back there in the caves forever. They'll start killing each other."

"We have time."

"How much?"

Wasn't that the million dollar question?

"We need to take it as slow as possible. Even with you picking from different towns, the humans communicate much more than they used to. They'll put it together eventually. The farther we spread it out, the less chance of detection we have."

She puffed her cheeks before releasing the breath in a huff. "You're right," she said, albeit begrudgingly. "But we also need to monitor the packs. You've given them a warning now."

"Logan's parents returned home today. I just saw it."

Raven's eyes met his, and there were a million questions swimming in her blue gaze. She pursed her lips, but just shook her head at him. In a smooth movement, she hoisted the body over her shoulder and made for the door. She stopped at it with her hand on the knob before she turned back to him.

"They are not the same, Xander," she warned. His spine locked straight at her presumption to speak about his past, but he knew she had a point. "She won't turn her back on Logan. She's his *mate*."

She left before he could open his mouth to retort.

Xander groaned, running his fingers through his hair. As much as he hated to admit it, Raven was right. Torian may intrigue him, may remind him of his past, but this would not play out the same.

Torian wasn't in love with him.

But...

The ideas spun in his head. Logan would see the similarities, the parallels between the situations, and Xander was sure they were already beginning to fester in the shifter's mind. *That* he could use.

He didn't have to make Torian love him. He just had to make her care. Had to make her hesitate in any situation where the vampire was involved.

He could do that.

Logan's parents were amazing.

Anyone with eyes could see the love they held for their sons. And it didn't take long before that warmth spread to envelope my pack as well. They made me feel at ease, which was surprising.

We were saying goodnight to everyone when Kenna pulled me into a hug.

"I'm so glad Logan finally found his mate," she whispered.

"Yeah," I said, forcing a smile onto my face.

"That's enough of that for tonight, Mom," Logan told her, coming to my rescue as if he'd sensed my discomfort. "Torian needs her rest."

Kenna's eyes hardened, but she pulled back and nodded. Logan and I had updated her and Nick on the situation with Xander earlier in the night. Everything from the war to the mark I now bore on my neck. His father was furious, and Kenna had turned frigid.

There was *definitely* more history between this family and that vampire than just the first war.

My eyes trailed down the hallway ahead of me. Ashlyn and Michael slipped into the bedroom they'd claimed for the duration of our stay, and I knew David and Rikki had already gone back to her room a few hours ago.

Which left me bunking with Logan.

There were worse things.

We went our separate ways when we got into the room. Logan into the bathroom, and I headed into the closet. Rikki had given me more clothes to hold me over until I got some of my own, and all I wanted was to change into something comfortable.

When I had changed into a pair of sweats and a t-shirt, I made a beeline for the bed. Falling into it, I snuggled down and left Logan as little room as possible. The water in the shower was running, and my eyelids felt heavy as I waited.

The creak of hinges startled me awake what could have only been a few minutes later. Fluttering my lashes open, I sat up on my elbows to face Logan.

I think I forgot how to breathe for a second.

All the asshole was wearing was a towel slung low on his hips, and my blood heated at the sight. My eyes snapped up to his, and there was playfulness dancing in the teal depths like sunlight on water.

Speaking of water, there was a droplet making a trail from the column of his throat, over his chest, before rippling over every defined abdominal muscle on display.

Gods, he wasn't even *fair*.

"Ma vie," he called, snapping my attention back to his face. He was beaming, and if he was closer, I might have smacked that self-satisfied grin right off his face.

"Don't you have clothes?"

"Somehow, they keep disappearing," he said, nodding toward the shirt I had on.

I glowered at him. So what if it was his?

He chuckled, and the deep, throaty sound made shivers race down my spine. The rustling of fabric met my ears, and then the bed dipped beside me as he pulled me tightly against his chest. I made a weak attempt to pull away from him, but inevitably just relaxed into his warmth.

His fingers trailed a soothing path up and down my arm, and it wouldn't take long to lull me to sleep.

Maybe having a mate wasn't so bad.

Logan may be a hothead sometimes, but he was also steady. Being here, with him and his family and his pack, I felt a sense of security that I don't think I *had* ever felt before. Surely not in my own upbringing.

That little black box rattled in the back of my mind, begging to break open.

Sleep. I just needed to sleep.

))))OCCCC

The cold registered first, like it was trying to creep directly into my bones.

I spotted the vampire sitting at the other end of the cot. He grinned at me, silver eyes shining.

"You know I could kill you, right?" I asked, moving into a sitting position. I glanced down. Still wearing what I wore to bed.

Thank the gods.

"You can try," he said, shrugging. "But I wouldn't suggest it in your current form."

Now that was an idea. Letting a coy smile dance across my lips, I closed my eyes and let the shift overtake me.

Only nothing happened.

Popping one eye open, I glared at Xander. He smirked, arching one elegant eyebrow at me. I slumped back against the wall behind the cot with a huff. His dream-vision thing. His rules.

I couldn't shift.

"What do you want?" I asked.

"Maybe I was lonely."

My eyes rolled, and I crossed my arms over my chest. Xander and I sized each other up, but he made no move to come any closer, which was appreciated.

I had little experience with older vampires. If we ever ran into them on our travels, they tended to be newborns. Unhinged and unpredictable. Xander was anything but.

Cold and calculated, I didn't think the vampire made many decisions without thoroughly thinking them out first.

Except marking me. That *had* been a last-minute decision, he had said. But why?

"I can see the gears turning in that pretty head of yours," he said, looking like he was fighting back a smile. "If you have questions, just ask."

"Because you'll be so forthcoming with information?"

"Try me."

My eyebrows raised. "Fine. What's the history between you and Logan?"

"His pack stole this land from us a long time ago. I want it back."

"You mean they ran you out after you refused to share the area?"

"Same thing."

"There's more to it."

"Perhaps." A growl built in my chest that I tried to force down. So much for getting answers. He was playing with me, and I didn't want any part of it. Xander tsked. "Careful now. Anything that happens to you here happens to you out there."

That got my attention. So I had to be even more mindful of how I acted around him in these dreams. Because I was nothing more than human, and if he decided to kill me, I'd die for real.

Distantly, I could hear Logan's voice. Xander sighed, and without another word, my vision went fuzzy.

Chapter Thirteen

"WHAT DO YOU MEAN?" Logan asked the next morning, running his fingers through my hair as I laid on his chest.

"He said anything that happens in the dreams happens here, too. I think it was a warning not to try anything stupid."

"Like trying to kill him?"

"Exactly."

Logan sighed, dragging a hand down his face before heaving himself to his feet. He snagged my waist and pulled me with him, pressing a kiss to my forehead before heading out of the room.

I took a few minutes to center myself while I got ready for the day. By the time I pulled another of Rikki's t-shirts over my head, I was composed as I could be.

David was the first to notice my presence when I made my way into the kitchen a few minutes later. His tawny eyes raked over me as he met me in the doorway. One look at my face had him pulling me into a tight hug.

"How're you feeling?" he asked, keeping his voice low.

Squeezing him back, I couldn't muster much more than a shrug. "I've been better," I admitted, pulling back from him. He held me at arm's length, brows raising. "I'm fine."

"Such a trooper."

He mussed my hair, and a half-hearted growl rumbled in my chest as I tried to smooth it back down. He grinned as he retreated to his mate's side. The smile that broke over my face couldn't be helped. Because seeing my second so happy, it was infectious. If anyone deserved happiness, it was David. The man who had had my back for more years than I cared to count any more.

Ashlyn appeared at my side, crossing her arms as she surveyed David and Rikki.

"You know it could be that easy for you, too, right?" she asked.

My head whipped to her so fast my neck cricked. Wincing, I rubbed it as I gaped at her. "Care to run that by me again?"

She glanced at me out of the corner of her eye, not even bothering to turn her head. "You heard me."

"So, Tor," Michael interjected, probably trying to save me from kicking his mate's ass. "Any plans for today?"

Not even thinking about it, I turned to Logan. There was a soft smile on his face, causing those teal eyes to shine in the early morning light. He stood a little straighter before opening his arms to me. The tug underneath my ribs was damn near physical, and I crossed the kitchen in a few steps. He enclosed me in his embrace, and I had to admit that Ashlyn had a point. The instant comfort that wrapped around me as his heartbeat thudded under my cheek was getting steadily harder to ignore.

"Would you all care if I took Torian out today, just the two of us?" he posed the question to my pack, but I knew it was just as much for me.

They waited for my call. Glancing up at Logan, I saw that he'd already fixed his attention on me. There was a challenge flaring in those eyes as they crinkled at the corners. Narrowing my own, I gave my pack a nod of approval.

I didn't know what a day alone with Logan would entail, but my curiosity was winning the battle.

"C'mon, ma vie," Logan said, entwining his fingers with me and tugging me toward the front door.

"Wait. Right now?" Pulling against his hand, I dug my heels into the floor.

"Yes," he replied, halting in his tracks to arch a brow at me.

Mild panic fluttered in my chest. Sure, I was curious, but I hadn't thought we were going to leave *immediately*. Some kind of preparation would've been nice. What did he even have in mind?

"But-"

"You've got three seconds before I haul you over my shoulder.

My jaw snapped shut with an audible click. "Excuse me?"

"One," he said, holding up a finger.

"We're really doing this?" I asked with raised brows.

"Two," he continued, completely ignoring me as his middle finger raised to accompany his index finger.

"Good luck." I placed my feet shoulder-width apart, ready for a fight.

"Three."

For a moment, neither of us moved. My eyes rolled, and I didn't have time to do much else before he struck. The air rushed from my lungs as he effortlessly tossed me over his shoulder.

"Logan," I hissed, swatting at his ass, which was obnoxiously close to my face. "Put me down."

"No can do, ma vie."

We were outside in a few steps, and the laughter of our combined packs filtered out after us before he closed the door. Logan took off at a brisk pace, away from the house.

"You can put me down now, Logan. I won't run."

"Promise?"

"For right now."

He chuckled softly before setting me on my feet. "Follow me, then."

I walked at his side as we approached the heart of town. It was a small town; the shop faces looking well worn as we passed by. Come to think of it, I hadn't been this far into town since the first day we arrived. My eyes trailed over everything, curiosity about the town's history and the man beside me burning through me. There was so much we needed to go over. I didn't even know where to start.

"So what're we doing?" I asked, deciding that was as safe a place to start as any.

"Shopping." Logan lifted one shoulder in a shrug before glancing down at me.

My eyes narrowed, but I refocused on our surroundings. The fact was that I *did* need clothes of my own, so I wouldn't fight him on this little expedition. This early in the morning, the streets weren't yet busy. Different shops lined the street we were walking down, but Logan seemed to have a specific one in mind.

I could see the streets branching off toward more residential homes as we continued on.

"Is that where the rest of the pack lives?"

Logan followed my gaze to the sprawling side streets before nodding. "Yeah, a lot of the younger shifters and their families live on this side of town. As they age and move up in ranks, they'll be eligible to move into the pack house if they want."

"So everyone there now is high ranking?"

"Pretty much. Dalton is my Beta, and Brooke is my third. Rikki has always been like family, so she moved in as soon as she was able. Troy moved in with Brooke as soon as their bond snapped into place."

"Why isn't Rikki your third if she's like family?" I wasn't touching the subject of mates with a ten-foot pole.

"Believe it or not, Rikki is all brute force. She's fierce on the field, but with Dalton and I already being hot-heads on our own, I needed someone level-headed to even us out. That's Brooke."

"Smart," I said. Because it was. I may have judged Logan too harshly that first day. He *knew* his pack, and himself. The makings of a great Alpha.

"Was that a compliment, ma vie?"

"Don't get used to it," I muttered, knocking my shoulder into his.

He rolled his eyes, but draped an arm around my shoulder and pulled me into him. My shoulders dropped on instinct as warmth rippled through me from the casual touch.

This godsdamn shifter hormone was going to ruin my plans.

"Here we are," he said, a smile in his voice as he motioned to the shop in front of us. The wooden sign hanging over the door read *Aunt Millie's Clothes and Apparel*. "It's the best place to get clothes here without going up into the city."

"It's perfect," I assured him. Just as he went to pull me through the door, I halted.

"Torian?"

"I don't have any money," I said, biting my lip. Shit.

"I can cover it."

"No, I can't let you do that."

"Please don't bother arguing with me on this." He sighed, grabbing my hand and all but dragging me the rest of the way into the store. "The others came up here days ago. You can't keep borrowing Rikki's clothes."

"But-"

"End of discussion, ma vie."

I harrumphed, but since I didn't really have a leg to stand on argument wise, I'd have to let him win this one.

The tinkling of a bell sounded as the door fell shut behind us. At the sound, a portly old woman rushed out from behind the counter.

"Logan!" she squealed with all the exuberance of a five-year-old. "It's so good to see you!"

Logan grinned, bending to her height so he could embrace her. "Hello, Millie."

She giggled and pulled away from him, brushing her gray curls out of her face. "And who is this?" she asked, her sparkling brown eyes falling on me.

"This is Torian," he said, stepping back to my side.

"It's nice to meet you," I told her, extending my hand. He hadn't introduced me as his mate, and that fact didn't escape me. I glanced at him out of the corner of my eye, and he just winked at me.

"Oh, I don't do handshakes, dear." It was the only warning she gave before yanking me down for a hug.

"Noted," I said, laughter bubbling out of my chest as she wrapped me in a surprisingly powerful grip. Shifter, then. I wondered if the whole town was, or if there were humans here, too.

"Well, Logan knows the store like the back of his hand. But if you need any extra help, don't hesitate to ask."

She bustled off, disappearing into a back room behind the register.

"She's so sweet."

"She's my great aunt," Logan said.

"Really?"

"On my mother's side. You should see her when Mom comes in here. She's nearly intolerable."

Laughing, I shook my head at him. "So why don't you tell me about this place?" I asked as I started flipping through the shirts.

"The store or the town?" I shot him a glare, and he beamed at me. "What do you want to know?"

"How does schooling work?"

"The same as it does anywhere, I suppose. There are just a few added classes on how to control your abilities," he explained, leaning one shoulder against the wall as he crossed his arms. "Speaking of school. How did that work for *you*, ma vie? Most nomads give up on it, depending on how long they've been on their own."

My back stiffened. He was treading on dangerous ground. But it was a valid question. He *knew* how long I had been a nomad. Sighing, I decided I could tell him some of it without fully delving into my past.

"I ran away about halfway through my sophomore year of high school," I started, my hands stilling in their flipping of clothes. "So no, I never technically graduated, but I did finally relent to David and get my GED."

That black box at the back of my mind rattled.

"Did the others do it too?" he asked, dragging me back to the present.

"David is relentless when he wants something," I said, shaking my head as a wry smile twisted my lips. "We didn't have much of a choice."

"He's not your Beta for no reason."

"Fair point."

"Any more questions?"

"How do you guys afford to live here?"

Those teal eyes tracked my movements as I went back to flipping through the shirts on the rack in front of me. "We've been here for ages. The properties pass through the generations, and most of our pack doesn't move on. If they do, the deeds get signed over to another family. The town is so small we've been able to keep it to just shifters, so we don't have to hide."

It made perfect sense. It was one of the major benefits of being in a large territorial pack. "You guys have it made, don't you?" I teased.

"Not without our mates," he replied. His playful tone let me know the dig was lighthearted, but it still felt like a bucket of ice water over my head.

"Logan…" I trailed off with a wince.

"Only kidding." There was an easy smile on his face, but it didn't fully reach his eyes.

"You're infuriating."

His laughter echoed around the small shop before he came to my side and helped me pick out clothes. Almost everything he suggested was so ridiculously hideous I couldn't do anything but laugh, which I think was his goal. There were a few items he was more serious about that I allowed him to put with the things I was buying. Well, *he* was buying.

With our arms full of clothing, Logan and I made our way to the counter once I was ready to check out. Millie's seemingly ever-present smile only widened when we set everything on the counter.

"Find everything okay?" she asked, grabbing her scanning gun to ring it up.

"Yes, ma'am," we chorused.

"Good," she mused, glancing between us with suspicion in her brown eyes. "You're not hiding anything from me now, are you, Logan?" she asked him, sounding like she already knew he was.

"No?" he said, his uncertainty making it sound more like a question. He swallowed audibly, and I had to bite my lip to keep from laughing at the panicked expression on his face as he dared a glance at me.

"Positive?" she pressed.

"Yes."

"Don't make me call your mother," she threatened, brandishing the pricing gun at him. Sweat beaded on his brow as his eyes danced back and forth between the two of us.

"I'm his mate," I told her, deciding I could save him, just this once.

She clapped her hands together. "I knew it!"

"He's just a little shy about it," I said with a teasing wink. Logan looked at me like I had three heads. I just shrugged at him.

Millie's tinkling laugh filtered around the store. "Oh, Logan! I'm so happy for you," she gushed, tears brimming in her eyes.

"Thank you, Millie," he said, his eyes never straying from mine.

"Well, you two probably have other things to do, so I'll just bill this to the house. That way you don't have to worry about paying now," she said, shoving everything into bags.

"Actually," Logan interrupted her, placing his hand over hers. "Why don't you just send everything to the house as well? If you don't mind," he suggested with that disarmingly easy smile of his.

"Oh, of course not!" she said, shooing us toward the door. "Go on, get out!"

"I feel like you did that so I wouldn't see the bill," I muttered a few minutes later as we walked.

"You feel right," he said, taking my hand in his.

Pulling it away, I narrowed my eyes at him. "I'll figure it out sooner or later."

"Probably later."

Cursing him incoherently under my breath, I allowed him to grab my hand again and intertwine our fingers. "We're going back already?" I asked, almost disappointed as I realized he was heading toward the house.

Logan chuckled, the sound carrying on the quiet street. "No. To the woods."

"Oh." Relief that I couldn't explain crashed over me as we turned off the road and started walking toward the trees.

A comfortable silence stretched between us as we made our way about fifty yards into the cover of the trees. Only then did Logan turn to me.

"Now, shift."

"What?"

His laughter rumbled deep in his chest at the indignation in my tone as he turned his back to me. He tossed his shirt off to the side, leaving his muscled back on full display.

"C'mon, Torian. Just trust me," he said, undoing his belt.

Heat rushed into my cheeks as I whipped around. The thing was, I did trust him. My entire body locked up at the realization.

When had that happened?

Chapter Fourteen

Even after all this time, the shift was still uncomfortable.

My eyes blinked open once I was sure I was on all fours. Logan wasn't far from me, his midnight fur gleaming in the afternoon sun.

"*There,*" I said, shaking out my own coat. "*Now, where are we going?*"

"*Trust, remember? Follow me.*" He took off at a dead sprint in the opposite direction before I even had a chance to respond.

My eyes rolled, but I only hesitated a moment before taking off after him. When I caught up with him, I adjusted my speed so that I was running in time with him.

"*You're not going to give me any idea what we're doing?*" I asked.

His laughter sounded in my head, and those striking teal eyes met mine for a heartbeat before refocusing on the path ahead of us. "*There's something I'd like to show you, but then I really don't care. I just wanted to go for a run. From the looks of it, so did you.*"

He had a point.

The wind blowing through my fur was a sensation that would never grow old. I couldn't believe how much I had missed it. Closing my eyes, I let myself go. I had become attuned to the beating of Logan's heart, so it wasn't difficult to follow him and his pounding footfalls. It could've been hours or mere minutes that we navigated those woods, but it ended all too soon.

But none too gracefully.

My eyes had still been closed, and it took me too long to realize that Logan had stopped. My body slammed into his, sending us both tumbling along the grass. He huffed as I came to rest on top of him. Shaking my head to dispel the fuzziness, I forced myself back to my feet.

It was hard not to gape as I took in the new clearing. While the terrain was different, I could tell it was the same stream we had crossed that very first day that cut through the ground ahead of me. The stream widened at this spot, its gentle flow interrupted by a small waterfall cascading from the far side of the clearing.

"It's beautiful," I told Logan. And that was putting it mildly.

"I figured you'd like it."

Glancing back down at him, the intensity in his eyes took me by surprise. Had we been human, I knew I wouldn't have been able to resist kissing him. As it was, I was safe in wolf form.

Trotting over to the stream, I stopped at the edge and looked down. As I met the eyes of my reflection, the little black box at the back of my mind burst open.

The memories surged forward against my will.

"It hurts!" I yelled. It felt as if every bone in my body was bending until it shattered.

"Hush, Torian," my mother, Camilla, said. Her voice was devoid of emotion, as it always was with me. "It'll pass."

"Jake!" The plea ripped from my throat and hot tears scalded my cheeks.

"It's alright, Rin," my brother said, clasping one of my hands in both of his. "I'm right here."

Another agonized cry broke free as my skin ripped and tore, changing from flesh to fur.

Finally, it all stopped.

I almost didn't hear the gasps as the rest of my senses flooded back.

"Rin, you're beautiful," Jake's voice echoed in my head.

Slowly, I opened my eyes and took in the area my family had brought me to for my first shift. Everything was in such greater detail, including the four other wolves surrounding me. Each one of them had a dark brown coat, though the shades slightly varied. Jake was the only one with a splash of white on his chest, allowing me to easily tell him apart from the rest of our family.

"That's... unexpected," my sister, Corie, said.

"What are you talking about?" It was as easy as talking, but still an adjustment.

"Just go look at yourself," my mother snapped.

A soft growl rumbled deep in Jake's chest as he glared at our mother before walking over to me. He bumped our shoulders together. "I'll show you."

Following him curiously, I stopped when he did at the edge of the water. Looking down, I almost jumped away from the sight of my reflection. My blue eyes were the same as always, but that wasn't brown fur covering my body.

It was stark white.

"That's me," I said, disbelief coloring my tone.

"Sure is."

"This isn't right," came my mother's irritated voice.

"Mom?" I questioned, looking over my shoulder at her.

The glare she sent me could've melted iron. She had always been cold with me, a little detached. But I had never thought it seemed like borderline hatred until this moment. Her eyes cut to my father, and he faced me. Something like regret flickered in his eyes before they steeled and I wasn't looking at my father anymore. The wolf before me was the Alpha of one of the largest packs in the country, and he radiated power.

"Jacob, with me." That Alpha's order echoed in my head, and Jake had no choice but to obey. Worry etched his face as he followed our father, only sparing a second to glance back at me.

Swallowing, I faced my mother and Corie. Corie was the oldest of us, and her eyes pinged back and forth between me and our mother.

"Things are going to change," *Mom hissed.* "No longer are you going to bring this family down."

"How have I ever-"

"Quiet," *she snapped, her eyes narrowing as she stalked toward me.* "You've always been different. Softer. This pack doesn't have room in it for liabilities like you." *Because I wasn't* like *them. Dad had always commended my compassion, but something had changed. I just didn't know what.* "I'm tired of watching your father coddle you. It's not doing this pack any favors, and it stops now."

Something inside me snapped.

My mother had always treated me differently than my siblings. Not that she was warm and fuzzy with them, by any means. She was slightly warmer with Jake than Corie and me, but not by much. I always chalked it up to maybe she had just wanted to be finished having kids before I came along, but enough was enough.

"Yeah, sure," I muttered, sarcasm dripping off the words. My mother glared at me for half a beat before shoving me into the stream.

The gasp that ripped free was almost the end of me. Water surged down my throat, trying to force its way into my lungs. My coordination in wolf form was still shaky with it being so new, and fighting my way to the air that lay above the surface of the water was a losing battle.

But I made it.

Choking and expelling water, I flailed until I reached the opposite side of the stream. It took every ounce of strength I had left to haul myself onto the grass, and I laid there heaving as I tried to catch my breath.

"You may not be as lucky the next time you disrespect me," my mother's voice invaded my head.

A bitter laugh fell from my mouth in a wolfish growl. She had tried to kill me.

There wouldn't be a next time.

"You know what?" I snarled as I rounded on her. Even though at least ten feet of water separated us, she took a step back in surprise as I bared my teeth. "If I'm such a disgrace to this family,

I'll get out of your hair. You can keep your precious little reputation, since it's so important to you."

But I knew better. I knew that she would have the fight of her life explaining to Dad, Jake, and the rest of the pack where I had gone. I trotted off toward the trees and away from all of it.

"Torian Vienna Pierce!" *her voice raged inside my head.*

I chuckled as I glanced over my shoulder at her. Corie stood dumbfounded behind her.

"I'm not a part of this family anymore, remember? Goodbye, Camilla.

)))))OCCCC

Logan's distant, worried voice finally penetrated the memory.

Hot tears tracked down my cheeks as I blinked, focusing on his face. His human face. He had me cradled in his lap, my naked skin flush against his, and mortification burned through me.

How long had I been like this?

"Ma vie, are you okay?" he asked when I finally mustered enough courage to meet his teal gaze again. Not being able to find my voice, I just nodded. He brushed my hair away from my face and kissed my forehead. "Do you want to talk about it?"

"Just a memory," I said, my voice coming out hoarse.

"A pretty bad one, by the looks of it." There was no judgment in his voice as he ran his fingers up and down my spine.

Fresh tears burned in my eyes, and I buried my head in Logan's shoulder to staunch the flow. But it was useless. I had kept the memories locked up and ignored for so long I had almost forgotten how much the flashbacks hurt. How much I missed my brother. Hell, even my dad and sister.

Sobs raked through me, and I couldn't even bring myself to care that Logan was seeing me like this. I couldn't keep track of time as Logan just held me, his arms tightening every once in a while. He was warm, and his wild scent that somehow reminded me of the ocean wrapped around me. Slowly but surely, I regained control of myself.

"Thank you," I murmured, rubbing under my eyes as I looked up at him.

"Anytime," he said, running his thumb along my cheekbone to catch the last errant tear that escaped. "Do you want to talk about it?"

My body stiffened on instinct, but I forced myself to relax. Logan was just worried about me. Meeting his eyes, I saw that worry swimming through them, and his lips pressed together in a thin line. Probably to stop him from pushing any further.

"Not now." Maybe not ever.

He nodded, his palm still cupping my cheek as he studied me. Sucking in a shuddering breath, I removed myself from his arms and shifted the moment I was clear of him. A soft sigh reached my ears, but Logan had followed suit and shifted as well by the time I turned around. We were right next to the stream still, and a wicked idea crossed my mind.

"*Logan...*"

Apprehension flared in his gaze. "*I don't trust that tone. What're you planning, ma vie?*"

"*Nothing.*"

And then I tackled him into the stream.

Chapter Fifteen

THE YELP THAT ESCAPED Logan was so high pitched it hurt my ears.

We resurfaced together, and I could almost feel his disbelief as he glared at me.

"What's the matter?" I asked, injecting as much innocence into my tone as possible. His brows arched, and I splashed more water at him. A growl rumbled from him.

"Now you're going to get it," he threatened.

"Catch me if you can," I taunted as I jumped back onto the shore. I was sprinting for the trees before he even touched the bank.

His cursing sounded in my head as he scrambled after me. It didn't take him long to catch up, so I zigzagged in and out of trees. Dodging a tall pine at the last second, I tried not to laugh when I heard him run into it headfirst.

"You'll pay for that one."

"All these threats, and I'm yet to see any follow through."

I just *had* to go and open my big mouth.

The full brunt of Logan's weight crashed into me only moments later. We fell in a tangle of limbs, and I snapped at his tail as it got a little too close to my face. His warning growl was low as he pinned me down, but the light in his eyes was unmistakable.

"*Alright, get off,*" I huffed.

"*Better?*" he asked, plopping down on top of me instead.

"*No,*" I groaned, kicking at him, to no avail. "*You're killing me.*"

He laughed before hopping up and moving away from me. I shook out my coat after getting to my feet. Glaring at him, I watched as he made the mistake of turning his back on me.

Grinning to myself, I snuck after him. Keeping myself low to the ground, I dodged any stick, rock, or leaf that might give me away.

I missed one, and the twig *cracked* under my paw.

When Logan glanced over his shoulder, I was already in the air.

He went sprawling across the ground when I slammed into his back, rolling us right through a patch of sticker bushes.

"*Shit,*" he muttered, as we skidded to a stop. He stood and tried to shake some of them loose. "*You're a menace today.*"

"*Wonder who's fault that is?*"

His eyes rolled before he turned and headed back toward the stream. Repressing the urge to mess with him anymore, I trotted after him. The walk back was quiet, both of us attempting to rid ourselves of the burrs that had gotten embedded in our fur. At this rate, our only hope was shifting.

"*Wait here,*" he told me when we made it back to the water. With a sigh, I made my way toward a boulder that had somehow escaped my attention the first time. The stream flowed peacefully beneath the massive rock, which jutted out like a cliff.

Natural steps carved into the earth led up to a level surface, beckoning me forward. Just as I was about to head up, Logan appeared again, his mouth filled with two baskets. He tossed one at my feet. "*Here.*"

Using my nose, I shoved the lid off to reveal the packed clothes. There were two sets, and I didn't bother questioning it as I grabbed the one obviously meant for me. Logan's eyes met mine when I went to turn. I rolled mine for good measure before going to change.

It didn't take long before the trees swallowed me, and I shifted back to human form. A few of the stupid burrs fell off, but I knew there were bound to be some stuck in my hair. Grumbling under my breath, I slipped the underwear on and examined the white fabric left in my hands. To my relief, it was a simple white sundress that no one other than Brooke would have picked out. Pulling the dress on, it pleasantly surprised me how comfortably the stretchy cotton fit.

Biting my lip, I walked back out into the clearing. Logan was already there. I wondered if the girls had packed his clothes as well, since he only had on a pair of shorts. My lips quirked up at the edges. His defined chest and corded arms were on full display, and I had to tamp down on the heat that rippled through me in response.

"Brooke's a genius," Logan said as I drew closer, verifying my earlier idea that she had picked out the dress.

"I knew you couldn't pick out something so nice."

With an eye roll, he closed the distance between us in three swift strides. He searched my face before cupping my cheek in his palm. When I didn't step back from him, his hand slid back until his fingers threaded through my hair.

And then snagged on a fucking burr from that sticker bush.

Both of us burst out laughing, and he spent a few moments helping me divest myself of the rest of them.

"That's what you get," he muttered as he threw the last one on the ground. He didn't waste any time before twining his fingers through the hair at the nape of my neck and angling my face up. His gaze dipped to my lips, and another piece of my resolve fractured.

Because in the short time I had known him, that mate claim had buried itself in my veins. Logan was made for me, and I felt it every single time he touched me. The longer I stayed, the more I allowed, the less I cared about denying it.

Logan made me feel innately safe. Which, if I was being completely honest with myself, was all I had really been searching for all these years.

His head dipped, but he paused a hairsbreadth away from my lips. Those teal eyes search mine, silently asking permission. Pushing up on my toes, I gave it to him as I sealed our mouths together.

"What happened to fighting me?" he breathed when we broke apart.

"It's become a very tiring process," I said before pulling him back to me.

The fire started as just a few smoldering embers, but as Logan encased my waist in his warm grip and tangled a hand in my hair, those embers ignited. Fire rushed through my veins, hot and fierce. My fingers knotted themselves into his soft hair, and

I pulled him impossibly closer. I couldn't focus on anything else besides the man in front of me. Logan was everywhere, and yet I still couldn't get enough of him as I molded my body to his.

Until another velvet soft voice broke through my bliss, shattering it.

ꆂꆂꆂꆂꆂ ꆂ ꆃ ꆃꆃꆃꆃꆃ

"Am I interrupting something?" Xander called, voice lazy as he eyed the shifters.

They broke apart, and it surprised him that the rumbling growl he could hear even from this distance came from Torian. Those crystalline eyes of hers flared when they met his, and he had to smother a smile.

"What are you doing here?" she hissed.

Xander tsked and held his hands up in front of him in a gesture of surrender. His eyes flicked to Logan, who stood behind her, observing. The tension in the male's shoulders was obvious, but Xander took note of the fact that he didn't push Torian behind him this time. Guess he had learned his lesson on that front.

"Hello to you too, Torian. I sensed you were out here," Xander said, inclining his head toward the mark she bore on her throat. The light reflected off the raised skin, and he could sense it pulsing in time with her heartbeat.

"So?"

It was a good question. One he didn't have an answer to. He hadn't been far when he had sensed her, and he had almost immediately altered his path. And even though he knew they were mates, quite literally meant for each other, it had still irked him to see them so enraptured with one another.

Xander had to remind himself that she was not his. And she never would be.

She was still waiting for his answer, brows arched. He cleared his throat before leaning against the tree beside him. "Figured I'd come say hi."

It was a lame excuse, and they both knew it. Torian blinked at him.

Logan watched Xander closely, trying to refrain from moving in front of Torian. She could hold her own, and he knew that. But the instinct to protect her was almost overwhelming. He briefly considered attacking the vampire, but even with the two of them, it wouldn't be easy. Either he or Torian could end up severely injured, and gods knew how much control Xander would have over her with his mark on her.

It wasn't worth the risk.

So Logan seethed, his anger roiling in his veins as the vampire stared at them. The longing in his eyes was familiar, and it made Logan's skin crawl to see it directed at his mate.

Xander had taken enough from him.

As the three faced off, they didn't notice the second vampire in the trees.

Raven perched on a branch, watching the exchange with narrowed eyes. Xander was flirting with disaster, and she didn't know if she could pick up the pieces of this war he had declared if the shifters decided to take him down.

Torian was what Xander had called the female. And as Raven examined her, Xander's fixation made sense.

The other vampire had a weakness for soft things. The difference here was that fire in Torian's eyes. She may look sweet, but even Raven could sense the girl's iron will. It was part of her gift. She could always sense how susceptible someone would be to her ability. And that woman in the clearing would take an immense amount of focus to influence.

Her mate, on the other hand, was already a raging ball of emotion, even if he had a pretty good hold on it.

Though before she could start meddling with Logan, Xander's head snapped in her direction.

His silver eyes narrowed in anger, and she just rolled her own in response.

Get back to the cabin, she thought, already knowing he was rooting around in her head. His nod of agreement was infinitesimal, and then she was gone.

Damn woman, Xander thought, refocusing on the shifters in front of him.

"As fun as this has been," Xander started, standing straight before turning his back on them. "I have places to be."

Raven had better have a good excuse for spying.

I watched as Xander disappeared into the trees. Logan's posture only slackened once the vampire was completely out of sight.

"Was it just me, or was that fucking weird?" I asked.

Logan chuckled, taking my hand and tugging me toward the other basket he had brought with him. An emotion I couldn't name still clouded his eyes, and I was once again reminded that there was some history between these two that I didn't know about.

But for right now, I wouldn't push it. Logan and I had been having a good day, and I wasn't about to let Xander ruin it.

We made our way up to the top of the rock I had spotted earlier, and Logan set the basket down once we reach the top. He pulled out a blanket and fanned it out so we'd be able to sit on it instead of directly on the hard rock. When he began to unload the basket, my eyes went round.

"Logan, you didn't."

He shook his head while laughter racked his frame. "No, I actually didn't," he admitted, continuing to pull out multiple tupperware containers. "The girls did most of it."

"So this morning, that whole asking for permission thing was what?"

"Strictly for your benefit," he said as an impish smile curled the corners of his lips.

"Asshole," I grumbled.

"You'll live," he said. He sat on the blanket and patted the spot beside him in invitation. For no other reason than to be difficult, I sat on the opposite side. It was his turn to roll his eyes as he snagged my waist and dragged me closer to him.

I couldn't help the laugh that escaped me. "Better?" I asked.

"Much."

Shaking my head with a soft smile on my face, I reached for a container holding strawberries. Before I could even get any, Logan snatched them from my hands. "Hey!" I protested, reaching for the container that Logan held out of my reach.

"This is supposed to be romantic," he admonished.

"Really? I hadn't noticed."

"Torian."

"What are you going to do? Feed them to me?"

"Maybe."

"Logan, no," I said, laughter creeping into my voice despite my best attempts to squash it.

He sighed before handing them back. "Fine. But if the girls ask, I tried."

"Deal." I popped a berry into my mouth to punctuate my sentence.

It didn't take us long to wipe out the entire picnic the girls had packed. Logan stretched out on the blanket. His eyes met mine, and he didn't even have to ask me to lie down next to him. My head rested on his shoulder as he idly ran his fingers through my hair.

"This is nice," he murmured.

I nodded, fighting the urge to close my eyes. The setting sun cast a golden glow as twilight settled in, and the clearing came alive around us. Fireflies danced over the stream below us, their lights helping to illuminate the place like millions of twinkling stars. Crickets chirped all around, and far in the distance, a true wolf howled its song to the rising moon. In those moments of near silence, it was as if Logan and I were the only two people in the world.

"Thank you for bringing me here."

"You're welcome, ma vie," he said, squeezing my shoulder.

A thought crossed my mind, and it was too good to pass up. Without a word to Logan, I tossed the sundress to the side and crossed to the very edge of the rock. My toes curled over the jagged edge, and I looked at the drop into the water. No more than twenty feet, if that.

"Care for a swim?" I asked, glancing at him over my shoulder.

There was heat in Logan's teal eyes that I, stupidly, hadn't anticipated. His gaze trailed down my body, and I thanked the gods the girls had thought to throw a bra and underwear in with the dress.

No different from a bathing suit, I reminded myself.

He stood, his movement slow. Measured.

I turned and jumped before he could take a step.

When I resurfaced, I heard Logan's curse, and then he was arcing through the open air. He landed with a splash mere feet from me. I lost track of him under the water, but his hands grasped my ankles and drug me under only a moment later.

I sucked in a breath just in time. The water stung my eyes a bit when I opened them, but I saw Logan grinning at me. And with his hair floating around him under the water, he looked so young and carefree. I didn't have a hope of staying any kind of mad at him. I just narrowed my own eyes and threw a sluggish kick at his shin before swimming for the surface.

"I hate you," I told him the moment we were above water again. He laughed, leisurely swimming toward me. I splashed him in the face when he was close enough. "Oops."

His grin turned wicked, and then the war was on.

I was at a tremendous disadvantage, so after a few minutes of getting bombarded with water, I was searching for an escape.

Logan swore when I sent the biggest wave I could manage at him, and I used his distraction to my advantage and dove. I made it behind the waterfall in record time and took in a few deep lungfuls of air.

"Ma vie?" Logan called, his voice muffled by the roar of the cascading water. That same water concealed the chuckle that slipped free.

It didn't take him long to figure out where I was hiding, and he popped up right next to me. I squealed, but he had his arms around me in an iron grip before I could run.

"Got you," he murmured, sending a pleasant shiver down my spine as his lips brushed against the shell of my ear.

"Don't think this makes you the winner."

"I wasn't aware we were in a competition."

I wriggled, and he just pulled me tighter against him. The hard planes of his chest were radiating warmth into me, and it was in stark contrast to the cool water.

I was a fool to have ever tried to deny this connection.

But the question still remained if I really wanted to let him all the way in.

To accept the claim in its entirety.

Chapter Sixteen

THE SOFT TWITTERING OF birds and sun on my face almost put me back to sleep the next morning. The brilliance of the clearing took my breath away once my eyes were open. Stretching my arms over my head as I sat up, I glanced down at Logan's still sleeping form. His bare chest made crimson creep up my neck as I remembered we had never gotten dressed after we finished swimming. Glancing around me, I spotted the sundress a few feet away. I reached over Logan to grab it and miscalculated how far I would have to stretch. The hand I was using to hold myself up slipped, and I fell face first onto Logan's chest.

He grunted before blinking his eyes open.

"Sorry," I whispered, wincing.

"It's alright. Good morning," he said around a yawn. He stretched as well, every corded muscle in his torso flexing. My mouth went dry at the sight.

"Morning," I croaked.

Teal eyes met mine, and he cocked a brow at me. He scanned my face, and then his gaze dipped lower. A slow smile slipped over his face, and he followed the direction of my outstretched hand. Chuckling, he grabbed the dress and held it out to me. When I took it from him, he snagged my wrist. He dragged me to him, our chests pressing together at the same time as his lips met mine.

My eyes slipped closed, and I threw all caution to the wind as I straddled Logan. A growl rumbled in his chest when he sat up, keeping as close as possible by banding his arms around my waist. My fingers tangled in his soft hair, pulling lightly. He grinned into the kiss, nipping my bottom lip.

Gods, when was the last time I had entertained the thought of getting lost in someone? I couldn't even remember.

His hands splayed across my nearly bare back before trailing up my spine, causing goosebumps to erupt over every inch of exposed skin. He was hard beneath me, and I reveled in the effect I had on him.

My hands slipped lower.

He threaded his fingers through the hair at the nape of my neck and pulled with enough force to break us apart. Both of our chests were heaving, brushing with every inhale as he pressed his brow to mine.

"Why'd you stop me?" I asked, leaning back just enough to breathe without his intoxicated scent assaulting me.

"Because the first time we're together, I want it to be with the bond in place. Preferably somewhere private."

My blood heated in answer. He knew he was going to get his way in the end, and I had to admit that it wasn't sounding so bad anymore.

Get your head out of the godsdamn gutter, Torian, I scolded myself. Taking a bracing breath, I climbed off of him. Yanking the dress over my head, I silently berated myself. At least one of us had our head on straight. If we would have slept together, the bond could've snapped into place all on its own. The magic mistaking the sex for full acceptance.

But wasn't that what he wanted?

My eyes strayed to the arrogant Alpha still sprawled out on the rock.

He had stopped me. Because he knew I still wasn't sure.

"Thank you," I breathed, feeling like I was truly looking at him for the first time.

His bright eyes glittered as he gave me that wolfish grin of his. Edged with irreverence, yes. But still so warm. So full of understanding.

I was royally, truly fucked.

He rose with a grace that wasn't even fair. "Are you ready to go home?" he asked, extending his hand in offer.

Home.

My whole body froze. Because somehow, in the short time I'd been here, that's what the pack house was. The first place I had felt content to return to since the day I left my family.

I placed my hand in Logan's, feeling the warmth that settled into my very bones as his fingers entwined with mine.

"Let's go."

Logan stopped long enough to grab the two baskets he had brought with us the night before, and then we headed for the house. Our hands swung leisurely back and forth between us as we walked through the awakening woods.

The house was in sight when every hair on my body stood on end.

Something was wrong.

Very wrong.

One look at Logan told me he felt it, too. The baskets fell to the ground as we both broke into a flat out sprint for the house. I made it first and wrenched the door open.

Crossing the threshold, I halted when I realized both packs had gathered in the living room. Nicholas and Kenna included. All of them wore identical expressions of grief. Logan appeared behind me and surveyed the scene as well. Taking tentative steps, I crossed until I could lay a gentle hand on David's shoulder.

"What happened?" I asked, my quiet whisper sounding like a gunshot in the deathly silence.

Nicholas turned toward me, his face looking old and worn. "They're dead," he said, voice flat. Lifeless.

I blinked a few times as my mouth went dry. Who?

"Who, Dad?" Logan asked my unvoiced question.

Nicholas stared his son dead in the eyes as he said, "Most of our pack."

My eyes widened, and I raised a hand to cover my mouth.

"How many?" Logan's hands were clenching and unclenching at his side, and his rage was palpable.

"Thirty-two," Kenna whispered.

My eyes widened in disbelief. Thirty-two?

Thirty-two?

How had so many been taken out so quickly? I could hear Logan speaking with his father, but my thoughts were swirling too fast to register much of what was being said. The words seemed like they were coming to me through water. How could this have happened? What monster could have done something like this?

A word from Logan and Nicholas's conversation carried to me. Vampire.

The realization hit me harder than a freight train.

Xander.

My back collided with the wall as I slid down it. Logan's eyes snapped to me, and he was in front of me in an instant.

"Ma vie, what's wrong?" he asked, his voice and eyes worried.

"Xander," I murmured, looking up into his eyes. It had to be. Maybe not alone, but he was raising an *army*. An army of vampires who would be hungry...

Comprehension dawned on Logan's face, and rage burned in his eyes.

"I'm going to kill that son of a bitch," he snarled, moving toward the door.

"Logan, no," I said, jumping up and rushing after him. When I grabbed hold of his arm, he glanced down at me. His teal eyes clouded over with malice, and I knew I had to talk him down quick. "Not by yourself. He's almost impossible to beat on his own. And he's *not* alone. It'd be a suicide mission."

Logan's eyes searched mine before he sighed in defeat. He slid his hand into mine, pulling me with him over to the couch. He sat me between him and David, who threw an arm over my shoulder.

An eerie silence settled over the room. It only took a few minutes before Ashlyn spoke up.

"How are we supposed to fight a war with only us?" she asked, voicing the question we were probably all wondering.

In those few moments, I made a hard decision.

Even though I didn't want to do it, we needed it.

Bad.

Standing from the couch, I made my way into the kitchen. Logan trailed after me as I picked up the landline phone with shaking hands. He placed his hands over mine, his warmth radiating throughout my ice-cold body.

"Ma vie, what're you doing?" he asked, searching my eyes. "What's wrong?"

Shaking my head, I pulled my grasp out of his and dialed the familiar number I had never quite forgotten. Putting the phone to my ear, I gave him what I hoped was a reassuring smile. "Nothing's wrong. Just calling in reinforcements."

Logan gave me a curious look, but didn't press the subject. Biting my lip, I listened anxiously as the phone rang.

Once.

Twice.

Three times.

Four.

They're not going to pick up...

"Hello?" the gravelly voice I had never hoped to hear again answered.

"Hey, Dad," I said, icicles dripping off the words.

Chapter Seventeen

THE SILENCE FROM THE other end of the line was deafening.

Logan's mouth had fallen open, so I reached over and shut it for him, offering a small smile.

"Torian?" I heard my father finally choke out.

"No. It's the tooth-fairy," I deadpanned.

"Where are you?" he demanded, trying to sound intimidating when, in fact, his voice was shaking.

"Somewhere in Virginia." I was feigning nonchalance, but my heart was pounding so hard I was sure the others could hear it from the living room.

He sighed. "You're so close to home..."

"That hell hole is not my home. Hasn't been in a long time."

"Torian, do not speak to me like that," he replied, matching the venom in my voice.

"Why? Because you're my *father*? Because I was treated so well while I was there?" My knuckles bleached white as I gripped the edge of the counter.

"Torian, I didn't know you were going to leave, but there's nothing I can do about it now." He sighed heavily into the phone. "And it doesn't sound like you're anywhere near forgiveness."

"No, I'm not. But I didn't call just to check in after all these years." Closing my eyes, I ground my teeth together. Whether or not I wanted to, I needed to do this. "I need your help."

"What kind of help?" he asked, apprehension creeping into his voice.

"The pack's help," I finally said after a few beats of silence. Logan wrapped his arms around me, and I leaned into him, thankful for his support.

Victor easily picked up on the weariness in my voice. "What have you gotten yourself into?" he asked.

Rubbing my temple with my free hand, I blew out a breath. I was going to have to let them back in.

Launching into the story, I walked him through meeting Logan, as well as everything that led up to meeting Xander.

He listened, not interrupting me once.

"He's wiped out nearly the entire pack here. Please, you know I wouldn't ask if it wasn't an emergency. I need the pack's help," I finished.

"Torian, do you know how hard it's going to be to–" There was a loud scuffling on the other end of the phone, cutting him off.

"Rin? Rin, is that you?" the voice I had missed so much echoed over the phone.

"Jake," I whispered, blinking furiously to stop the tears that were threatening to overflow. He must have picked up one of the other phones in the house.

"It is you!" he yelled. "You're alive! Are you okay? When are you coming home? Or are you even coming home? I miss you so much, Rin," he rambled.

"Jacob!" our father barked.

"Sorry."

"Now," Victor started. "Do you know how hard it's going to be to uproot a pack this size?"

"Yes, I do. But we will *not* survive this without help." My fists clenched of their own accord. "Please, do this for me. Show me you're sorry, if you even are."

The silence that followed as he made his decision nearly killed me.

Jake was the one to break it.

"C'mon, Dad. Ever since she left, you've been wallowing, kicking yourself in the ass for letting her get away." I called bullshit, but kept my mouth shut. "You know you want her back home. Admit it or not, but you miss her as much as I do," he said, his voice growing soft toward the end.

"When do you need us there?" Victor asked.

"As soon as possible. Riverview, Virginia," I said as an ear to ear smile broke out across my face.

We were going to be okay.

The clicking of keys sounded down the line as he looked up the fastest route from his home in Tennessee to where I was in southern Virginia.

"We can be there by tonight," he said.

"Thank you," I whispered, not quite believing it.

"Of course," he replied before clicking off.

"Rin?" Jake asked, his childhood nickname for me nearly bringing tears to my eyes again.

When I was born, he had apparently always said *Torin* instead of *Torian,* so he had just taken to calling me Rin. The name had always stuck. Apparently, even now.

"Hey," I said.

"Why're you suddenly calling?"

"I need your help, Jake," I admitted, clutching the phone in my hand so hard I feared it would break.

"What's going on?" he pressed.

"My mate's pack is in deep with a clan of vampires and a war is coming. There's only a few of us, Jake. We can't do it alone."

"Dad was right. We'll be there as soon as possible. In fact, I'll be the first one there. Love you, Rin."

"I love you too, Jake," I whispered. "Bye."

I clicked the end button and slowly set the phone down on the counter, bracing myself against it.

It was done. They were coming.

After everything, I was going to let my family back into my life.

It's to save all of us, I reminded myself. With that thought in mind, I raised my head to meet the shocked stares of the others.

"I think you have a little bit of explaining to do, young lady," Nicholas said.

Logan encased my hand in his as I took a steadying breath. Gathering my thoughts, I met the eyes of every shifter in the room. After they found out about my past, about who I was, everything could change. Or nothing would.

I was hoping for the latter.

The thing was, for almost a year after I ran away, search parties were sent out. They had almost every pack in the continental

U.S. looking for me. Hell, it wouldn't have surprised me to learn my father had alerted shifters globally to his errant daughter's disappearance. There had been a high reward for my return home.

Two years passed without a trace of me, and my family had assumed I was dead. All searches stopped.

That was when I had found David.

I met Kenna's eyes and readdressed the question she had asked me the first day I met her.

"My full name is Torian Pierce. I'm the runaway daughter of the Tennessee Pierce pack," I announced, watching the shock and confusion play across the expression of almost every wolf in the room. "I left for a multitude of reasons, but being called a disgrace on the night of my first shift was my breaking point. So, I took what I had left of my dignity and I ran." My fists clenched again as I stared at the granite countertop that was threatening to buckle under my hold.

"I was fourteen when I set off on my own," I continued, my eyes flashing up to meet David's. He gave me a warm smile that I couldn't help but return. "I found my pack slowly after the searches stopped. Even though we were nomads, we knew we needed a leader. The Alpha blood in my veins ran strong, and we made the decision that I should embrace it. Not that it gave me much choice.

"I have never backed down from my duties to protect my pack. If I'm required to call upon harsh memories and unwant-ed help, so be it. The safety of those around me comes first. We need help to win this war or else we'll *all* die. We need them to survive." My head fell into my hands as a shiver skittered down my spine. "They'll be here at some point tonight."

The silence was deafening, and I stood rigid as I waited for their response.

Finally, Nicholas spoke. "You're Torian *Pierce?*" he asked, sounding completely awestruck.

"Tor, you didn't have to call them," David said to ward off the oncoming awkward silence.

"Yes, I did. You *know* we needed their help."

"But–"

"What's done is done," I said with an air of finality, my Alpha tone creeping into my voice against my will. Sighing, I addressed the group. "I know this is a lot to take in, but they'll be here before we know it." Turning to Kenna and Nicholas, I bit my lip. "I guess I technically should have asked you guys first. Do we have room to house them?"

"We'll accommodate them, Torian. You don't even have to be anywhere near them if you don't want to," Kenna said. She shook her head before coming around the counter and pulling me out of Logan's arms into her own.

"She's right," Logan said, placing a hand on my shoulder as I snuggled into Kenna's motherly embrace, something I wasn't exactly used to. "You can hole yourself up in our room if you don't feel you can face them."

"Our room?" I questioned with a quirked eyebrow, turning to gaze into his calming teal eyes.

"What's mine is yours, ma vie," he said, wrapping his arms around my waist and drawing me back to him.

"That was so corny," I chided as I wrapped my arms around his neck.

"That was the idea," he whispered, leaning his forehead against mine. Someone cleared their throat, and I immediately jumped away from Logan. He laughed, but kept my hand securely in his. Blushing, I realized it had been Dalton. He was grinning ear to ear.

"I take it back, kid," I said, narrowing my eyes at him. "I don't like you so much."

"Doesn't bother me." He shrugged.

Silence descended, and the grief came with it.

"I'm going to go talk to the families," Logan announced, his arms tightening around me for just a moment before releasing. "They deserve to hear from us, and I want to assess the damage myself."

"Do you want me to..." I trailed off, not knowing if it was even my place.

But Logan's eyes shone with tenderness. He ran his thumb along my cheekbone as he shook his head. "This is my pack, and something I need to do alone."

I nodded, leaning into his touch for just a moment. And then he was gone.

Blowing out a breath, I turned to the others. Ashlyn came forward first, wrapping her arms around me in a tight hug.

"We'll be right here with you," she whispered, pulling back so that she could hold my gaze. David and Michael stepped closer as well, somber expressions on their faces.

They knew the whole story. Knew about how my mother had almost killed me that day, intentionally or not.

My heart swelled as I took my pack in. I couldn't imagine losing a single one of them, and Logan had just lost *so* many.

I didn't think I could survive it.

A flash of red in my peripheral caught my attention. Rikki slipped her hand into David's as she came up beside him. Her hazel eyes met mine, and she offered a small smile.

"Why don't you stick with us for today?" she asked, nodding toward Brooke.

"I think that's a good idea," Ashlyn said, not even giving me the time to answer. I shot her a dirty look, but followed them back to Rikki's room all the same.

David stayed behind with Michael and the others.

❨❨❨❨❨❨❩❩❩❩❩❩

The girls and I excused ourselves back to Rikki's room just after we finished dinner.

"Kenna is *such* a good cook," Rikki said, collapsing onto her bed. Brooke, Ashlyn, and I all piled on as well until we were practically falling off.

I nodded my agreement, rubbing my overly full stomach.

"I'm so glad you two came around," Brooke said, motioning between Ashlyn and me. "It's nice to have some other girls in the house."

"I'm sure all that testosterone got irritating," Ashlyn quipped.

"You have *no* idea."

"So," I started, looking at Rikki and batting my eyelashes. "How are you and David doing?"

"We're great. He's amazing." She met my gaze. "He worries about you a lot. About Logan."

All eyes were suddenly on me and I bit my lip as I stared at the covers. "Um..." was I all could manage.

"C'mon, Torian. What happened on your date?' Brooke pressed, trying to bite back a smile.

Of course, they would want all the details. With a soft sigh, I launched into the full story. From meeting Millie, to the picnic, to the stream. I glossed over the run-in with Xander. We didn't need another reminder of the atrocity that had occurred.

"And then we went to sleep," I finished.

"That's it?" Brooke asked, giving me a funny look.

"We kissed?" I said, my cheeks tingeing pink.

She shrugged. "I just figured Logan would have tried to go farther—Ow!" she yelped as Rikki slapped her arm.

My eyes narrowed. "Care to share?"

Rikki glared at Brooke, who just grinned sheepishly. Rikki sighed, shaking her head before she spoke. "Logan was not exactly the most innocent before you came along. He was so disappointed about being an unmated Alpha, he thought there was something wrong with him. So, he made some shitty choices."

"He's grown up a lot," Brooke chimed in. "He's gained the respect of every wolf in this pack. I think everyone understood where he was coming from."

Little did they know, I knew exactly what they were talking about. I *was* an unmated Alpha. It was like there was a piece of me missing. But I had always ignored it.

"It's in the past," Brooke said, her big blue eyes pleading. I blinked at her. Did they think *this* was what was going to make me reject the bond?

"Guys, calm down," I said, laughing. Rikki and Brooke's mouths dropped open, and Ashlyn just smirked. "I never expected him to be a saint. What he did before he even knew about me won't change the way I feel about him. It's not like I'm some pillar of modesty either." I shrugged. "I trust who he is now."

"You trust him?" Ashlyn asked, her voice barely more than a whisper.

"Yeah. I do." My cheeks tinged scarlet under her narrowed gaze. Instead of the lecture I had expected, Ashlyn threw her arms around my neck and squealed. The pillow I hit her with cut her off. "Shut up."

All three of them laughed, but Ashlyn refused to let go of me. She looked like a weight had lifted off of her. For the first time, I wondered if she had been worried about me the same way David was. She caught my stare, and her ocean eyes glittered as she grinned at me.

A few hours later, I sensed Logan return. It wasn't something I could really put a finger on, but something in my chest settled, and I just knew he had returned home. I fought the urge to go find him, and let him have the time I knew he needed to decompress from the day.

But once darkness fell, it wasn't long before Logan knocked on the door. He stuck his head in, motioning for Rikki to turn down the music we had on.

"There's some guy I don't know in front of my house. He's a shifter, and he's alone," he said, his voice somewhere between seriousness and amusement.

"Jake," I breathed.

I was on my feet in an instant, running down the hall to the front door. As a last-minute decision, I checked myself in the mirror by the door, wanting to look at least somewhat presentable. Taking a deep breath, I wrenched the door open and stepped out into the night.

Chapter Eighteen

THERE HE WAS. ALL six foot four of my older brother.

He smiled ear to ear when he saw me. Within seconds, he wrapped his muscular arms around me, nearly crushing me. He spun me around in a circle while I laughed, hanging onto him for dear life.

"Jake... can't... breathe," I gasped out.

"Sorry, Rin!" he said as he set me back on my feet, holding me at arm's length. "God, you've grown."

"And you dyed your hair?" I asked, reaching up to ruffle his blonde locks.

He shrugged, absently running a hand through it. "The whole 'uniform perfection' thing was really starting to piss me off." He had said it with his familiar crooked grin, and my heart seized in my chest. My eyes flickered over every feature on his face. The strong jawline, high cheekbones, and chocolate eyes were pretty much exactly the same as they had always been.

"I missed you so much," I murmured.

"Ditto, kid."

"Shut up." I punched his arm. "I'm only two years younger than you."

"Gods, it's good to see you," he said, laughing as he pulled me into another bone-crushing hug.

A throat cleared behind us, causing me to pull back from Jake. Logan stood a few feet behind us, arms crossed and eyebrows raised. His eyes traveled from me, to the bottle blonde at my side, and he dipped his chin in acknowledgment.

But he still had his feet braced like he was squaring up for a fight.

Men.

My eyes rolled so hard it almost surprised me I couldn't see the back of my skull. Logan caught me, and his lips twitched up in amusement. Holding my hand out, I raised my brows at him.

He took the invitation and made his way over, tucking me into his side once he was within range. Jake tracked every movement, his eyes calculating as they slid back to mine.

"Jake, this is my mate, Logan," I said. Mischief flashed in my brother's brown eyes, and I kicked his shin. "Be nice."

"Jacob Pierce," he introduced himself, glaring at me the whole time. "So you're the one who got stuck with Rin, huh?"

"Hey!" Why had I missed him, again?

Logan just chuckled. "I am. Logan Grey. It's good to meet you."

"She's a handful," Jake warned, smiling as he gave me a knowing look. "Take care of her."

"You two ought to get along just fine," I huffed, shrugging away from Logan. "You both think I'm some fragile little doll that needs to be handled with caution." Jake opened his mouth to retort, but the sound of heavy footfalls cut him off.

My mouth ran dry as I whipped my head up to face Logan. I'm sure he meant the small smile he offered to be reassuring, but I knew him better than that by now. The corners of his eyes were tight with worry, which didn't help my mini anxiety attack.

"They're shifting," Jake murmured just loud enough for me to hear as he came to my side.

Logan's front door creaked, and I knew without looking it was the rest of our packs coming out to join us.

David moved to flank my left, and Logan wrapped his arms around my waist from behind. Everyone else filtered in. Some of my worry ebbed away as I drew strength from having my pack near me.

My father was at the head of the crowd when they emerged from the trees. My mother and sister were right behind him. They had always been ones for making a grand entrance, so they were walking toward us in a pyramid formation. My father's eyes found mine, and we stared at each other as the entire Pierce pack continued to advance on our small conjoined one. As they halted not even ten feet away from us, Logan squeezed my waist tighter and placed a feather-light kiss on my neck.

When my father spoke, his voice was somewhere between irritation and relief.

"Torian," he said with a curt nod of his head.

"Victor." I forced a smile. One glance at my mother's look of contempt conveyed how much she wanted to be there.

"You should feel privileged that your father even had the compassion to come all the way out here to salvage yet another one of your useless messes," she snarled.

So we were starting with hostility. Wonderful.

"It's great to see you too, mother," I replied in a sugar-sweet tone with a broad smile. My gaze moved to my sister, and I had to blink a couple times to verify that it was tears I could see shining in her eyes. "Corie."

"Torian..." her voice cracked, and I tried to keep the surprise off my face.

"She'd never admit it, but she missed you, Rin," Jake said as he leaned down to my ear. He spoke so low, I knew he was trying to keep his voice from carrying to our family.

"Torian," my father called, distracting me from what Jake was saying. "Introductions?"

"There are two packs here," I began, jumping right into it. Why was this always my job? I rattled off the information about both packs gathered and then waved my hand toward my family. "Of course, that's the Pierce pack. Questions?" I asked, nudging Jake in the ribs when I heard him laugh.

Rikki reached around David and tapped my shoulder. "We're okay with the blonde one, right?" she asked.

"Unfortunately," I replied, stifling my laughter.

"Tor?" a tentative voice called out. Lifting my head, I found it was Corie who had spoken. Those tears still glazed over her brown eyes as she fought to hold them back. "I'm so sorry."

Her voice was so sincere, so filled with pain, it made my eyes widen. Shrugging Logan's arms off me, I crossed the space between the two groups until I was right in front of my sister.

"Cor..." I trailed off. She glanced up at me through her eyelashes as silent tears escaped, only to roll down her face. That was all it took to break me. "I forgive you."

With a choked sob of relief, she threw her arms around me. "It's so good to see you," she mumbled against my shoulder.

"You too," I told her as I returned her embrace.

"Corie," our mother snapped. "Dry those tears. You will not show any weakness." At her words, Corie slowly pulled away from me and Camilla sneered. "Especially not in front of *her*."

"Why are you here?" I asked, rounding on her with a snarl. "If you hate me so much, you didn't have to come."

"Where Victor goes, I go. So keep your trap shut."

"You don't control me anymore, Camilla."

"Maybe not. But your Alpha does," she said, sounding so damned proud of herself as a smirk curved her lips.

"Good thing I'm my pack's Alpha, then." Her eyes went wide with shock and the color leeched from her face. I grinned in response, a sick satisfaction running through me as I watched her struggle to gain the upper hand again.

"But–"

"*But* if you don't want to be here, I give you the option. Leave," the longer I continue to speak, the harder it was to keep the Alpha command out of my voice. Control and self-preservation had never been my strong suit, so I threw caution to the wind and drew myself up to my full height. "This is not your territory. You have no authority here. Neither does Victor. So, stop with your petty shit. You can stay and help, or you can get out."

Technically, I couldn't order her to leave. Only Logan could do that. But I needed her to understand that I wouldn't be falling back in line just because I had asked for help.

"I'm not leaving," she hissed, malice dripping off of every word.

My entire body bristled. The warm hand on my shoulder kept me from spewing the vitriol I wanted at her. Logan's calm, teal eyes met mine when I glanced back. He lightly squeezed, and all the anger dissipated in an instant.

However, it seemed to simply transfer to Logan if the glare he sent my mother was anything to go off of.

"I don't care who you are, Mrs. Pierce. You will not speak to my mate that way on my land. If you insist on doing so, I will personally remove you," he said, his voice deadly low. My eyes widened at the dark expression on his face.

It was new, this side of him. But the anger rolling off of him was palpable. I don't think he'd even looked at Xander with the kind of loathing he was leveling at my mother.

Victor turned to Camilla with a sardonic smile twitching at the corners of his lips. "What're you going to do now, *dear?*" he asked, irritation buried deep within his tone.

"Don't patronize me, Vic," she said as her entire body shook. "If the little bitch wants me gone, let's see her stick up for herself for once in her life."

My temper blazed again, wracking my frame with the force of holding back the shift.

"What is your *problem?*" I asked her.

"You."

And then she lunged for me, a snarling brown wolf in her place.

Chapter Nineteen

ABSOLUTE SHOCK WIDENED MY eyes, but in the next breath, I was shoving Logan away from me.

My shift tore through me, but I barely registered it as I jumped out of Camilla's way. She landed in front of Logan, right in the area I had occupied only a second before. Small gasps sounded from the Pierce side as I shook out my coat. Guess they had forgotten I didn't have a speck of that dark brown coloring that favored all but Jake.

My mother rounded on me, her teeth bared as she snarled, "*You're a pathetic excuse for a wolf.*"

It was a fight not to roll my eyes. Nearly eight years had passed, and she was still spouting the same shit.

When she lunged for me, I braced myself and let her tackle me. We tumbled, and I growled when she pinned me beneath her. I had underestimated how much bigger she was. Saliva dripped off her maw, and I curled my lips back from my teeth before going for her throat.

She dodged at the last minute, jumping off of me and backing away. I huffed out what could pass for a laugh as I circled her, watching her hackles raise as she tracked me.

"I'm so pathetic," I mused, testing her reflexes as I switched directions, *"yet I've still got you on the run."*

The taunt worked.

When she lunged for me again, it was sloppy. Satisfaction whipped through me as I met her in the air.

And this time I was the one that came out on top.

The leash I had kept on my anger for all these years was slipping. She was the reason I had lost my family. She was the reason behind every contention. *She* was the reason I had to grow up too quickly. To take a position that was never meant to be mine.

"You were a mistake," she said, her voice hissing through my head. *"I could sense it from the moment you were born. A mother just knows these things."*

"You're a pathetic excuse for a mother," I retorted, twisting her own words. With a snarl that rattled the surrounding trees, I sank my teeth into her shoulder.

My vision was going red at the edges, both from the blood and my own rage. Ripping out a chunk of her flesh, I moved off of her as her pain filled howl rang out. She whimpered as I darted around her and bit into her leg.

She kicked me off her, standing on shaky legs to face me. Hatred flared in those brown eyes, and for a split second, I wished I could understand it.

"You were a threat to Jacob being Alpha."

The words stopped me in my tracks.

"What?"

We circled each other once again. I knew she was waiting for an opening, and probably hoping that her declaration would throw me off my game. And it was working.

"*Your father and I are not mates,*" she told me, her eyes darting to the man in question. It was something I had always known, but had almost forgotten about. "*It was a marriage of convenience, since neither of us ever found our mates. A marriage for power. In my bloodline, white fur is the mark of a leader. Of an Alpha. The more of it, the stronger the wolf.*"

My eyes darted to my brother, remembering the splash of white that decorated his chest when he was in wolf form.

"*Jake was always meant to be Alpha,*" I said, my brain trying to make the pieces fit with what I knew about my childhood.

"*Two great Alpha lines combining to create one of the strongest shifters this world has seen. And when Jacob was born, I just knew. Knew that* my son *was going to be the next great Alpha of the Pierce pack. On the night of his first shift, I saw that beautiful mark on his chest. It was exactly as I had hoped for.*"

It made sense. Why she had always been so distant from Corie and me. All she wanted was to produce the strongest heir. In our world, that generally meant a son.

But then-

"*And then you had your first shift,*" she said, as if she were finishing my own thoughts. "*And your* entire *coat was white.*"

"*I never would have wanted it.*"

"*I wasn't taking that risk.*"

She moved faster than I had been expecting. She had been playing weak, and I fell for it like an idiot. Her teeth sank into the soft spot between my neck and shoulder, and I heard Logan's roar as blood spilled.

My eyes darted in his direction, and I saw Jake and David holding him back. He was shuddering with the force of containing his shift. Our eyes caught, and I shook my head at him.

I needed to do this alone.

Focus, I told myself, ripping free from her.

The wound tore wide open, and I couldn't stop the whimper that slipped free. I didn't have time to acknowledge the pain. Not with the way she was looking at me. My blood streaked her muzzle, and I tried to ignore the hunk of white fur that had fallen at her feet.

I stopped moving, cocking my head to the side as a thought occurred to me. *"Does Victor even know?"*

"No, not about the markings."

"Now who's pathetic?" She snarled at me, the sound low and vicious. "Leave," I ordered, advancing on her. *"If Victor wants to take the pack with you, so be it. I never would have taken Jake's title from him, but I became an Alpha anyway. I have people I need to take care of, and if you're not here to help, then you're wasting my time."*

We stared at each other, both of us bleeding from the wounds we had inflicted, and unfiltered rage flitted through her eyes before she shifted back to her human form.

"We're leaving, Victor," she called, turning to him and crossing her arms over her bare chest.

"No," he said, rolling his eyes as he ran a hand through his hair.

Camilla bristled. "What was that?"

"I said no," he repeated. "My daughter needs our help. I'm not sure what went down the night she left, but I'm starting to think I may not have gotten the full story. If you want to leave, I'm not stopping you. Any of the pack that wishes to go back with you is welcome to."

She stared open-mouthed at him for a full minute before rounding on me.

"You'll pay for this," she threatened, marching over to me and getting in my face *again*.

Rolling my eyes, I snapped my jaws at her.

She jumped away from me, and I followed, herding her into the woods. Her back collided with a tree trunk and she sent me one last glare before shifting. She ran off into the night, not looking over her shoulder once.

The dumbstruck faces of the packs caught my attention when I turned back around. The anger ebbed away, and I realized I had done it. I had faced Camilla and *won*.

Suppressing the urge to let out a howl of victory, I walked back to Logan. He grinned at me, pure pride glowing in those teal eyes.

In wolf form, we were the same size as the animals we looked like, so I had to jump in order to nudge his shoulder. He quirked an eyebrow before realization dawned on his face.

"You need clothes, don't you?" he asked. I nodded, and he stripped his shirt off in an instant. He swung it around my neck so that I'd have it when I shifted. "There."

A sound of thanks rumbled in my chest before I turned to head into the tree cover. As I passed by the large bay window that gave a view of Logan's living room, my reflection caught my attention. Unable to help myself, I winced. Splotches of mud and deep crimson stains dotted my snow-white coat. I didn't even want to look at my shoulder, so I forced myself to take the last step into the woods.

The changing of bones caused me to grit my teeth as my shoulder changed form, reopening the already semi-closed wound. That was a problem for later, since it may take a day and a half to fully heal, anyway. Pulling Logan's shirt over my head, I caught sight of the mud that covered my hands. A bone-deep sigh escaped as I raised the hem of the shirt to swipe at my face. I got off as much as I could with the dry cloth before heading back to the others.

Logan was sprinting for me the minute I cleared the trees.

"You did amazing, ma vie," he murmured in my ear, pulling me against his chest. For just a moment, I let myself revel in his warm embrace.

Drawing my shoulders back, I caught his eye and winked before I turned to face my father's pack.

"Any of you that wish to leave with Camilla are more than welcome to," I started, giving them the same out my father had. "Very few of you know me, and none of you have any obligation here. We are fighting an immensely powerful vampire, and he doesn't like the idea of losing. He's building an army, and though I hate to say it, deaths are certain." I allowed my eyes to sweep over the crowd. "There's no need to risk your lives here if you are not willing."

"We're here to protect the Pierce bloodline. You're a part of that," a man somewhere on my left called. Others around him echoed the sentiment, and no one made a move to follow in my mother's tracks.

"Alright then. We'll find you places to rest so we can all get some sleep. We'll start going over plans tomorrow." Murmurs of agreement rippled through the crowd and Logan wasted no time before pulling me toward the house with him. A wave of exhaustion crashed over me, and I allowed myself to lean into his strength.

"Tired?" Logan asked as Kenna and Nicholas moved in to divide the Pierce pack amongst the town.

I nodded, and a wide yawn escaped me. "Answer your question?" I muttered as my family and our packs entered the house behind us.

"C'mon then," he said as he towed me down the hall.

"Rin!" Jake called, stopping us in our tracks. "Where are you going?"

"To bed."

He jogged down the hall until he was right in front of me. "Together?" he asked, his eyes flicking to Logan.

"Jake, I may be your little sister, but I'm not a kid anymore," I reminded him with an eye roll.

"The older brother in me wants to threaten to rip your throat out if you try anything, but I think she'd beat me to it," he told Logan, crossing his arms over his broad chest.

Logan grinned, glancing at me out of the corner of his eye. "Oh, she absolutely would," he said. He didn't give Jake a chance to respond before he pulled me into the bedroom and shut the door. "Protective," he muttered, watching the door as if it would burst open at any second.

"He hasn't seen me since I was fourteen," I reminded him, laughing softly. "It's a lot to take in."

"I understand. He loves you." He cupped my face, running his thumb over my cheekbone. The movement was familiar, lazy, and it caused some of the tension to drop from my shoulders. A small grin played with the edges of his lips before he bent and sealed them with mine.

Home. This was what home felt like.

The realization clanged through me, and I blinked as he pulled away.

As his teal eyes bored into mine, I thought about how easy it would be to simply give in. To accept that bond that writhed beneath my skin like a restless viper.

But everything with my family was so fresh, I needed time.

More time that I didn't know if I really had.

"What're you thinking about?" he asked, not moving an inch away from me.

Shaking my head, I retreated. His eyebrows quirked, but he didn't push as I brushed past him into the closet. I grabbed a change of clothes and made a beeline for the bathroom. The door clicked shut as I pressed my back against it, trying to control my ragged breathing.

I was going to throw myself into a panic attack.

A sharp cry tore out of my throat as I whipped Logan's shirt over my head.

"Son of a bitch," I spat, letting out a string of curses under my breath.

"Ma vie?" Logan called, knocking lightly on the door. "What's wrong?"

"Nothing," I said, grinding my teeth together as I jerked the shirt off. "Hold on a second." Wincing, I reached over and grabbed a towel to wrap around myself. I examined the vicious bite mark that took up practically my entire right shoulder in the mirror. Fresh blood ran over my collarbone, and I swiped at it to keep it from staining the towel. The old blood must have fused with the shirt and come off with it, reopening the bite.

Again.

The wound was trying to stitch itself back together, but it was so wide it would take forever if left alone. My eyes flicked to the closed door. Sighing through my nose, I let my head drop back so I could stare at the ceiling.

There were two options. I could call Dr. Walker, or I could let Logan help me with it.

"Come in," I grumbled, crossing my arms over my chest. He thankfully heard me and peaked his head in.

His eyes went wide when they caught mine in the mirror. "Why aren't you dressed?" he asked before his gaze zeroed in on the bite mark. "Oh," he breathed, coming in and shutting the door behind him.

"It happened during the fight," I said as he came closer. Being this close to him in a half-naked state was causing a blush to creep up my neck to settle in my cheeks.

"I saw." He kept his voice low, and as if he could sense my discomfort, he tried to restrain a grin. "I've seen you in less," he reminded me, moving my arms so that he could get a better look at my shoulder.

"What? When?" But of course he had. When I had the flash-back, and shifted in the midst of it. This time, my entire face flamed scarlet.

"Let's just focus on this right now," he said, trying and failing to keep the laughter out of his voice.

"Fine." The blood from the wound was dripping onto the floor, and I cringed. "Logan..."

"I'll get it after I take care of you," he told me, reaching past me and opening the medicine cabinet. He pulled out a roll of gauze before turning and snatching another towel off the rack. He turned the warm water on and held the towel under it before pressing it to my shoulder. I hissed in pain and tried to jerk away from him, but he braced my other shoulder so that I couldn't move. "I'm sorry."

"You're fine," I said between gritted teeth. "You think it'll need stitches?"

He watched as the magic that ran through every shifters veins tried to force the skin to heal. But he must have come to the same conclusion I had, because he nodded. He tapped my hip, and I moved out of the way of the vanity. He squatted, rummaging through the contents until he found a small first aid kit. Setting it on the counter, he pulled out a needle, thread, and a couple butterfly bandages.

He jerked his head toward the shower. "Get in."

"Excuse me?"

"You're filthy, ma vie," he pointed out, his eyes flicking over every speck of dirt that still clung to my skin from the fight. "I know you don't want to sleep like that."

Grumbling unintelligibly under my breath, I did as I was told. Logan laughed and then shed his own clothes.

"*What* are you doing?" I asked, whipping my head around to face the wall. Not before I got an eyeful of what was between his legs, but I was trying to ignore that.

His deep chuckle was suddenly much closer, and I felt his warm skin press against me. I clutched the towel tighter as his lips brushed my ear, sending a shiver down my spine.

"I want to help you, but if this is too much, if you want me to leave, just say the word."

I opened my mouth to do just that, but the words wouldn't form. He ran the back of his hand down my arm, and I released a shuddering breath.

Fuck it.

The towel slipped, and I silently held it out without looking at him. He pressed a kiss to the back of my uninjured shoulder before tossing the towel over the curtain rod. His entire front pressed against my bare back, and the smallest gasp escaped as he leaned past me to turn the water on.

The spray from the shower hit me square in the face, and I flinched back into him. He chuckled before backing up to give me room. Grabbing a washcloth and soaking it in the warm water, I took a deep breath before turning to face Logan.

His eyes locked onto mine, and even the pain in my shoulder faded to the very back of my mind as we gazed at each other.

When he took the cloth from me, his hands were shaking.

"This is going to sting," he warned, his deep voice rasping more than usual.

And sting it did. I hissed and scrunched my eyes shut as he cleaned the wound. He murmured words of encouragement the whole time, and I tried to focus on the sound of his voice instead of the cloth slipping lower.

Logan's strokes were sure and methodical as he removed all evidence of the fight from my flushed and burning skin. The cloth brushed against my hip, and my lashes fluttered open as Logan knelt in front of me.

Every thought eddied out of my head.

He glanced up at me, his unruly hair curling over his forehead as the water weighed it down. The look of absolute reverence in those teal eyes was almost my undoing.

"Logan," I murmured.

He stood, gently nudging me back until I was standing under the spray. The *crack* of the shampoo bottle opening echoed through the room, and my eyebrows raised as he squeezed some into his palm.

"Head back," he instructed. I didn't bother arguing as his fingers threaded through my hair. He massaged my scalp, and the moan that slipped past my lips was indecent. A low growl rumbled in his chest. "Torian," he warned.

"Sorry," I whispered.

He huffed out a laugh and quickly finished washing my hair for me. In a matter of moments, he had rinsed the suds out and turned the water off. He wrapped the towel back around me and stepped out first before slinging another around his hips. He held his hand out for me to take, and my eyebrows lifted.

"Ma vie?"

"I have a bite wound. Not a broken limb."

His eyes rolled, and he just picked me up by the hips. I squealed as he sat me on the vanity.

"Let me do this."

"Fine." His smile softened as he threaded a needle I hadn't even noticed him grab. "Have you done this before?"

"Many times," he admitted, flicking his eyes up to mine. "I don't like bothering Dr. Walker with little stuff, so I taught myself."

"Stitches are *little stuff?*"

"Deep breath." It was the only warning he gave me before pinching the skin together and piercing it with the needle. A litany of curses left my mouth, but the pain was manageable. Logan's shoulders shook with his laughter, but his hands stayed steady. It was only a matter of minutes before he was tying the end of the thread off and wrapping gauze around my shoulder.

"Thank you," I said, grabbing his hands as he went to put everything away. "For everything."

"Whether or not you want to admit it, ma vie, you are *mine*. To protect. To care for. And to stand beside in all things. I don't know what went down between you and your mother today, but something told me you needed to be taken care of for once." He shrugged as if it were no big deal, and my heart constricted.

A comfortable silence fell over us as he helped me dress. His words from before floated back to me, as he entwined our fingers together and towed me toward the bed. That he didn't want to sleep together until the bond was accepted.

And damn if tonight didn't prove that. Even though he had me in my most vulnerable state, not once did I think he was going to push for anything more.

Because, to my utter horror, Logan was *good*. And I truly had no hope of denying the mate claim in the long run.

Shit.

Chapter Twenty

Raven studied the small cabin from her seat at the table. Her knife spun beneath her finger, its tip digging into the table-top.

Xander could move anywhere. He had the power to do, quite literally, anything he wanted. Yet he still kept fighting for this same scrap of land. Raven couldn't understand it.

She shook her head. It was pointless.

"It's my *home*, Raven," his lazy voice called.

She jumped, not expecting Xander to show up so soon, let alone be listening to her thoughts while he was at it. Placing a hand over her slow-beating heart, she took a deep breath to brace herself.

"Don't sneak up on me like that," she muttered, glaring at him.

A cruel little smirk tilted his lips as he leaned one shoulder against the cabin wall. The picture of ease, but she could tell he was still furious with her. His silver eyes flashed as he clicked his tongue. "I have every right to sneak up on someone who is in my home, uninvited."

She rolled her eyes, fighting the urge to throw her dagger at him.

His quirked eyebrow was a dare.

"Be as mad at me as you want, but it was a good plan," she told him, using the tip of her blade to point in his direction. "Albeit a little short-sighted."

"You thought taking out over half their pack with a few rabid newborns wouldn't have repercussions?"

"Not like this."

That got his attention. He pushed off the wall and came closer. The room seemed to shrink little by little as he stopped mere feet from her.

Gods, she still hated the effect he had on her.

"Explain."

"Torian isn't as much of a loner as you initially thought." She worried her bottom lip between her teeth. He was going to kill her. "She's a Pierce. *The* runaway Pierce, to be exact."

Xander's entire body went still. Those quicksilver eyes settled on her with a predator's focus, and she uneasily got to her feet, palming her dagger. She edged around the table, placing it between them as she held her hands out in a placating gesture.

"And how do you know this?" he asked, his hands flexing at his sides as if he were contemplating wrapping them around her neck.

"They're here."

He lunged so fast she didn't have a hope of seeing it coming.

Her knife slid into his side, but it didn't even faze him. He did, indeed, wrap his fingers around her throat as he shoved her against the wall. Her feet didn't reach the ground from where he was holding her, and she clawed at the constricting hand.

"How many?" he hissed, briefly glancing down to glare at the hilt of her knife sticking out just below his ribs.

"The entire pack, from the looks of it."

"Give me one reason I shouldn't rip your head from your body right now." He pressed harder, and she feared he may crush her larynx before she could get the words out.

She tapped against his hand, and he snarled before dropping her. She crashed to her knees, coughing as she tried to catch her breath.

"Because I can still help," she croaked, hating the tears that blurred her vision. "You know I still hold sway over the newborns. And I can broaden my hunting grounds. Turn more."

Xander paced, running his fingers through his dark hair. Raven didn't bother trying to stand. He needed to cool off, or she'd just find herself fighting for her life again. And the next time, he might not keep his powers out of it.

"We need to start training the newborns immediately," he told her, finally coming to a halt. "The longer the shifters have to train, the harder the fight will be."

"Do you want to contact any of the others?" she asked, referencing the other vampires that had fought in the first war. "Maybe with their help-"

"No," he cut her off, head shaking. "I told you, I reached out to most of them before coming to you. They didn't want to help then, and I won't debase myself by begging." His eyes met hers, looking like they were lit from within as the sunlight spilling through the windows caught them. "You and I will win this."

She pulled herself to her feet before crossing to him. He held perfectly still as she grabbed the hilt of her dagger. She ripped it free, only thinking about gutting him with it for a split second.

The look in his eyes said he had heard it.

Xander watched her go, feeling his anger ebb with every step she took. The move against the pack had been foolish, but there was nothing to do about it now. All that was left to do was make the most of the hand they had been dealt.

But the Pierce pack was an obstacle he had never expected.

He wasn't an expert on shifters by any means, but everyone in their world knew about the Pierce pack. They were strong and had been for eons. Their line went back longer than Xander cared to remember, and they had held their territory for just as long. In numbers alone, the vampires were now likely outmatched.

Which was why Raven got to keep her head. Because she truly was the best for the job.

His mind drifted, settling on a pair of startling crystalline eyes, and he had to shake the thoughts of Torian from his mind. Even now, he could sense her. He knew she was asleep, and it was all he could do not to invade her dreams. He desperately wanted to, but he knew it wouldn't play out well. She likely had pieced together the truth of what happened with the rest of the pack, and no doubt blamed him.

Which wasn't entirely incorrect, so he couldn't blame her.

It also meant she probably wanted his head on a stake.

The next time he saw her, he'd explain. And apologize. Because having her in the middle of this whole feud caused a tightness in his chest he didn't want to examine.

She was incredible.

Logan held Torian closer to him, her head on his chest, the next morning. He idly ran his fingers through her hair, letting a smile play across his face. He couldn't believe that even amid everything that was happening, he was still happy.

It almost seemed wrong, when so much had just gone wrong with his pack. He knew that the families that had lost someone would all do their own funerals and services, and as Alpha, he would attend every single one in the coming week.

But he had found his mate. And Torian was everything he could have ever envisioned for himself. She was so strong. He still couldn't fully wrap his head around her calling in her family. To put the sake of a pack that wasn't even her own above her own needs, it was nothing short of incredible.

Logan just feared she was handling it *too* well.

It had only been a matter of weeks since Torian showed up. And in that time, she'd had a mate, a psychotic vampire, this war, and her family all thrown into her life. Most people would've buckled under the pressure.

But not Torian. She was just taking it in stride.

It was part of why he was so thankful she had let him dote on her last night. *Something* beyond what they could see or hear had gone down during the fight with her mother. He should have shifted. That way, he could've heard the conversation. But the thought had come to him too little, too late.

He blew out a breath as he tightened his hold ever so slightly. She may have her own secrets she was holding close to her chest, but Logan had things he hadn't shared with her yet either...

His thoughts trailed off as Torian stirred, cuddling deeper into his chest before her eyes fluttered open. Her crystal blue eyes instantly caught and held his attention.

"Morning," she whispered, a sleepy smile crossing her face.

"Morning," he greeted, leaning forward to kiss her forehead. "Sleep well?"

"Completely vampire free," she told him with an enthusiastic thumbs-up.

"That's something I'll always be happy to hear."

She laughed, the soft sound warming his heart as she sat up and stretched. She winced, dropping her arms immediately to glare at the spot where the bandage hid beneath her shirt. A few curses flew from her lips as she prodded at the bulky dressing.

"Damn thing," she muttered.

"Take your shirt off," he said. The wound should have been damn near healed by now.

Torian's eyebrow quirked at the request. "Logan," she protested.

"It's just so I can get a good look at it, ma vie," he assured her, cupping her cheek in his palm.

Her eyes softened as she nodded. She let him help her ease the shirt off before holding it across her bare chest. He swore as he inspected the bandage, only to find that it was almost soaked through.

"What're you doing?' she called as he got up and headed for the bathroom.

"I'm going to need to re-bandage it," he replied. He wet a cloth with warm water and grabbed the roll of gauze before returning to her.

"Oh."

"This may hurt," he warned, beginning to remove the old bandage. She nodded, and as soon as he unraveled the gauze, he heard her teeth grind together. He tossed the bloody bandage into the trashcan beside the bed and wiped the wound clean. His shoulders slumped at the sight.

The skin had, thankfully, fused back together. A yellowing bruise decorated the entirety of her shoulder, but the wound itself had scabbed over. Logan figured if they were lucky, it would be gone by the end of the day.

"Good news or bad?" she asked, and he realized she was staring at the wall.

"Good." He removed the butterfly bandages from the night before, since they were no longer needed. Just to err on the side of caution, he rummaged around in his nightstand drawer until he found the healing salve Dr. Walker insisted he kept on hand. The minute he unscrewed the cap, the scent of the potent herbs stung the air. Torian's nose scrunched as she whipped her head around to see what he was doing.

Logan chuckled, dipping his fingers into the salve before smoothing them over her injured skin. When a low hum of approval left Torian's throat, he wished he would've thought of it the night before. He carefully reapplied the gauze, but this time he didn't wrap it as tight. She should have a better range of mobility with it now.

"Should be gone by tomorrow," he said, brushing a kiss over her cheek as he got up to return the supplies to the bathroom. When he came back to the bedroom, Torian was already heading out the door.

"You coming?" she called over her shoulder. He nodded before trailing after her as she made her way to the kitchen. She busied herself by rummaging through the cabinets as Logan plopped onto a stool at the island.

"Ma vie, what're you doing?" he asked, a smile tugging at the corners of his mouth.

She set a frying pan on the stove. "Familiarizing myself with your kitchen," she said, not even bothering to pause in her exploration.

"Why?" he asked, placing his elbows on the island counter and resting his chin in his hand.

She stopped for a moment and looked back at him, her eyes sparkling in the early morning sunlight pouring in from the window. "Because I'm the first person up that knows how to cook, and I'm going to make breakfast."

"Are you saying I don't know how to cook?"

"Are you saying you do?" She arched her brows, pulling milk, eggs, and butter out of the refrigerator.

"Yes."

"Then why don't you make yourself useful?"

"Maybe I like the view," he murmured, not bothering to restrain a coy grin. Her head lifted, and he saw the exact moment his words registered. Her face flamed scarlet, and she gave him an acidic glare before turning her back to him.

"Well, too bad," she said. She spooned some of the batter onto the griddle she had plugged in. "Get your lazy butt up and help. I'm cooking for fourteen here."

Chuckling, he stood and made his way over to her and began helping her prepare a big breakfast for their combined packs. Logan couldn't help but sneak glances at her out of the corner of his eyes. The east-facing window above the sink was allowing the full brunt of the sunrise to wash over her. Logan wasn't paying a bit of attention to what he was doing, and he sliced his finger with the knife instead of the peppers he had laid out.

"Ow, shit," he said, letting out a string of other profanities under his breath as he dropped the knife and walked over to the sink. He was running the cut under cold water when Torian raised up on her tiptoes to glance over his shoulder.

"What'd you do?" she asked, amusement buried in her tone.

"Cut myself," he grumbled, tearing a paper towel off the roll. He wrapped it securely around his finger, knowing it would heal within minutes.

"And how'd you manage that?"

"You distracted me..."

"Maybe I shouldn't have let you cook," she mused, a wide grin splitting her face.

"Probably not," he said with a laugh, tossing the paper towel in the trash. Sighing, he returned to the stool he had formerly been sitting on. Torian moved to the coffee machine and started a pot before moving back to the griddle. She flipped a full batch of pancakes onto a plate and slid it onto the middle of the counter. Logan reached for one, and she smacked his hand with the spatula, wielding it like a weapon.

"Wait on everyone else," she scolded before turning back to the griddle and placing another batch.

"Fine," he said. He watched as she plated everything else and laid it on the counter alongside the pancakes. Once she had turned around to the stove again, Logan slowly reached for a piece of bacon.

Something smacked him on the head, and he glanced down at the plastic fork that had just settled onto the counter. Wide eyed, he looked at Torian's back.

"I said wait," she told him without even turning around.

"How did you know?"

"Female instinct," was all she said as she glanced over her shoulder at him.

He grumbled something unintelligible under his breath and her tinkling laugh filled the quiet room. Logan couldn't help but smile as he watched the easy way she moved around the kitchen, almost as if she had been there all her life.

She'll make a great mother.

The sudden thought had him about falling out of his chair.

The mating instinct showing itself this early was alarming. But the thought had already passed, and it was leading to more. Visions of Torian's stomach expanding with a pup of their own, or just her brilliant smile as she served breakfast to their family. Logan had to shake his head to clear it. He couldn't be having these thoughts so early into the relationship, if that's what this even was. Torian wanted to take it slow.

Logan figured it'd be best to keep those thoughts to himself for now. It was already hard enough to fight the pull toward her every single time she was within arm's reach.

Chapter Twenty-One

THE PLATE HISSED ACROSS the counter as I slid the last batch of pancakes into the center.

When I glanced up to meet Logan's eyes, he was already watching me. Not that his focus wasn't always on me in one way or another, but the intensity in those teal eyes caught me off guard.

Blinking repeatedly, I raised a hand to my face. "What?" I asked. He stood and made his way around the counter. He stopped when his toes touched mine, and he framed my face in his hands.

"You're absolutely beautiful," he murmured before covering my lips with his. Sighing, I slipped my arms around his neck at the same time one of his snaked around my waist, pulling my body flush against his.

"Holy shit!" a familiar voice squealed. Turning my head, I caught sight of Ashlyn in the kitchen doorway. Her hand was covering her mouth, and I rolled my eyes at her theatrics. When she dropped it, a smirk that I didn't trust in the slightest danced across her features. "I walked in at just the right time. Another minute and you two would have set off the smoke detector."

"Ash, shut up," I hissed, struggling to keep my blush under control as I broke away from Logan.

"Why the hostility?" my bottle-blonde brother asked, walking into the room as if he had timed it. Sending Ashlyn a warning glare, I set a cup of coffee in front of her in offering.

The mischievous grin she shot me said she couldn't be bought.

"I walked in on your sister and her mate about to fuck on the counter," she told him, batting her eyelashes.

Jake choked.

"What?" he sputtered, jaw dropping open. With a sheepish smile, I slipped behind Logan.

"Want some coffee?" I asked my brother, poking my head out from behind Logan. To enunciate my point, I placed a steaming cup of coffee in my mate's awaiting hands.

"You're avoiding the question, Rin."

"I don't know what you're talking about," I said. Gods above, *why* had I wanted my brother under the same roof as me again?

"What did Ashlyn walk in on?" he pressed, rolling his eyes as a smile spread across his face. Good to know he still delighted in annoying me.

Ashlyn snorted.

"She walked in on me kissing my mate," Logan said, sounding exasperated. He threw Ashlyn a look that could have cut glass, and I didn't even feel sorry for her.

Jake surveyed Logan before his gaze slid back to me. That playful light in his eyes didn't bode well for any of us.

"Help yourself," I said, cutting off whatever had been about to come out of his mouth.

Without waiting for any kind of response, I turned on my heel and headed for the door to the backyard. Leaning my head against the cool glass, I blew out a breath. Having everyone under the same roof was going to be a struggle. Maybe I had bitten off more than I could chew this time.

The sounds of the rest of the house waking up and trickling into the kitchen filtered to me as if through water. Logan told them to help themselves to the meal I had prepared, and then his light footsteps sounded as he came up behind me. He wrapped his arms around my waist before setting his chin on my good shoulder.

"You okay?" he asked, keeping his voice low enough not to carry.

"It's a lot," I admitted. "I don't think I've really processed everything yet."

"Take it at whatever pace you need to. I'm right here if you need me."

My hands settled over his, and I squeezed them in thanks. He stood straight again before spinning me around to face him. His lips brushed over my brow in a reassuring kiss as he towed me back toward the counter where everyone else was loading up their plates.

"Now, let's eat," he said, handing me a plate.

The soft laugh that fell from my lips released the tension I hadn't fully realized had knotted in my shoulders. Logan helped me fill my plate until I was certain there was more food than I could eat. His was just as full as he carried both into the dining room with everyone else.

Logan set my plate down at the head of the table and took the seat to the right of it. Eyeing him with raised brows, I didn't fight it as I took my seat.

When I looked at the packs surrounding the table, the reality of it all slammed into me.

They were all here.

My pack. Logan's. My family's.

There was still a darkness over the house with the loss we had endured, and it caused a roiling in my stomach. Pushing through the feeling, I nodded to everyone and started eating. The clicking of silverware sounded through the room as everyone else followed suit. Logan placed his hand on my knee under the table and gave it a reassuring squeeze before picking up his own fork.

"It'll be fine," he murmured without looking up. He sounded so sure, and I could barely breathe properly.

Some Alpha I made.

"Torian," I heard my father's voice call from somewhere down the table.

My head raised to search for him. He was about halfway down the table and watching me expectantly. I regarded him, trying to block out the conversation that had transpired between my mother and me the day before.

He had still let her push me away. Had still taken Jake with him that night. He may not have deserved as much blame as I originally placed on him, but he wasn't innocent.

But I had to swallow my pride for now. Cooperation was going to be necessary if we wanted any chance of ending this war with the vampires.

"Yes?" I asked, finally acknowledging him.

"I know it would be ideal to adjust to having the pack here. You all have been through a horrendous tragedy, and need the time to grieve. But we also need to train as soon as possible. Who knows when they'll make their next move?"

I hated how right he was.

I turned to Logan, and he was already watching me. This was his pack. His call.

"Some of us can be ready as soon as today," he said, turning to face my father. To his credit, Victor met Logan's gaze head on. "I would venture to say everyone in this house is ready. But I won't force the families of the fallen to participate if they're not up to it yet."

Logan's gathered pack all nodded, and mine looked to me. I almost rolled my eyes at them.

"We're ready," I said. Logan smirked as if he had already known that.

Which I'm sure he had.

"The clearing we first fought in?" Logan asked, tilting his head in my direction. Jake's head whipped up, and I just held a hand up to stop whatever question was on the tip of his tongue.

"That should work. After breakfast?"

"Any objections?" he called as his gaze slid around the table. Everyone shook their heads, and with Logan's nod, everyone went back to their previous conversations. My mate turned back to me, silent worry reflecting in his eyes as he settled his hand back on my knee. "Are you sure?" he asked.

"This is my fight now, too," I reminded him as I placed my hand on his cheek. "I'm in this until Xander's either dead or surrendered."

He shook his head at me despite the smile now adorning his features. Placing his hand over mine, he turned his face to place a tender kiss on the inside of my wrist.

"Thank you, ma vie," he murmured, his voice turning to silk.

"Anytime," I whispered, turning back to finish my breakfast.

)))))⟩OC(((((

The group from the pack house and some of the Pierce's best fighters were all in a circle surrounding Logan and me.

Looking around at our fighters, I had to hold back tears at the thought of losing any of them. Just as Logan had predicted, most of what remained of his pack had decided against training just yet.

But us, the warriors, we would fight to avenge our fallen. And we would welcome anyone who wanted to help once they were ready.

"Alright!" Logan called out, hushing the quiet buzz of conversation into an expectant silence. "Now I know we all have different fighting techniques," he began, resting his eyes on each member of the three packs present. "The best way I can see to go about this is to pair off with someone from another pack and teach each other the skills we each hold."

"How can you possibly learn to fight better than a Pierce?" a muscle bound male from the Pierce pack sneered. I bristled at the intended insult layered deep under the man's snide tone. Logan opened his mouth to reply, but the instinct to defend my mate had me speaking before he even had a chance.

"I just took down your Luna last night," I reminded him, crossing my arms over my chest. "It's obviously not that hard."

"You're a Pierce," he said dismissively, waving me off.

"I hate to break it to you, but I've been absent from the Pierce family since the night of my first shift. I never learned the *proper* ways and fighting techniques that my father has taught you." He had the good sense to look sheepish, but that didn't stop me. "What I know, I learned myself from being on the run and fighting for my life. *I* honed every skill I have on my own. So, go ahead. Tell me that what I know is because I'm a Pierce," I threatened, my voice so low I wasn't even sure it would carry to him. "I dare you."

"I won't fight a female," he said between gritted teeth, turning his head away from me.

"Too afraid I'll hand you your ass too?" I taunted, rearing for another fight to relieve some of the stress that had piled up over the past few days. "If you think that there are only going to be male vampires to fight, you're sadly mistaken."

"I'm not afraid," the man said, stepping forward as my father watched from a distance with light amusement dancing in his eyes. "You've got yourself a fight, kid."

He disappeared into the trees to shift, and I whirled to do the same. Logan caught my arm just as I was about to slip into the cover of the surrounding woods.

"Be careful, ma vie. He's big," Logan cautioned. Rolling my eyes with a laugh, I tried to shake his hand off, but he wasn't budging.

"You and Mike are probably just as big, and I do just fine against you two." Worry still creased his brow, so I leaned up on my tiptoes and brushed a kiss across his cheek. "You're never going to be able to fight this war if you're worried about me the whole time. Focus. I'll be okay," I whispered in his ear before pulling back to meet his gaze. He sighed through his nose, nodded, and released me.

Grinning, I slipped into the tree cover. I was eager for the fight. It was an adrenaline rush like no other, and a much needed distraction. Shedding my t-shirt and jeans on the forest floor, I quickly deposited my undergarments with them. Bones, muscle, and tissue reformed themselves as I let the shift overwhelm my body until I could shake out my fur.

There was a hulking mass of a wolf waiting for me when I returned to the others. He stood nearly a head and a half taller than me and the lean muscle that lined every bone in his body made me look like an ant next to him. Despite all that, his sandy-brown fur was thick and fluffy, almost making him look like a stuffed animal.

Taking my place about twenty feet away from him, I sank into a crouch. The bite mark Camilla had left me with twinged, but it was practically healed now. I wasn't worried.

"*What's your name?*" I asked, my tail wagging in the air. He sank down to mirror my position, but his demeanor was anything but playful.

"*Lee,*" he growled. "*Torian, right?*"

"That's the one."

"Torian," Logan called, causing me to raise my head in his direction. He stepped between us. "On three," he said. "One. Two. *Three.*" He hesitated only a millisecond before stepping out of the way.

Lee studied me for a few beats, and I didn't dare make the first move.

He cocked his head and sidestepped to the right. The moment his paw twitched, I had already darted left. My ability to know how my opponent was going to move the second they did had always been something I prided myself on. So, when Lee experimented with going left, I moved right. Keeping low to the ground, I was on the lookout for any sign of him lunging. But he just continued to practice with my reflexes before I finally saw his muscles coil.

The minute he was in the air, I was sprinting to the other side of the clearing. He landed, and confusion danced across his face when he whirled around to face me.

"You're fast."

"You have no idea," I replied as I slowly prepared to spring.

"So are we going to play cat and mouse all day or-" My body slammed into his, sending him crashing to the ground and cutting him off. Grunting, he jerked away from me and walked back to the other side of the clearing. *"It's on now, kid,"* he taunted, lowering into a crouch with a slight wag of his tail.

"Broke through that tough guy exterior that quick, huh?" I asked, mimicking his position.

He barked out a laugh with a shrug of his massive shoulders. *"I have a soft spot for people that gain my respect. But no more going easy on you."*

"Bring it on."

That was all the invitation he needed.

Within seconds, he had cleared the area between us and tackled me to the ground like he was pushing over a paper cup. Growling, I kicked him off me with my hind legs. The maneuver caused me some pain, but it was worth it. Wincing, I followed his flying form. I didn't give him a chance to recover once he landed. I pounced on him and snapped my jaws close to his face. He grunted, knocking me off of him and pinning me under his weight.

Wriggling, I made one of his paws slip. My teeth closed over his leg in the next instant. He growled, and I kept myself from drawing blood at the last second. He withdrew, and I was just about to lunge for him again when his voice echoed in my head.

"I give, woman," he said, before shifting back to human form. A defeated smile stretched across his face as he turned and disappeared into the trees again.

That had been way too easy. There was no way he had been trying.

Despite my theory, I trotted back over to Logan. I was too lazy to shift back, so I just laid down beside him instead.

"So is everyone clear on how this is going to work?" he called. Everyone nodded in agreement, and he did a quick headcount. "Looks like we have an uneven number. At least one person is going to have to sit out now and then. Who's going to sit out first?"

"Me," Corie said, raising her hand. "I never was a very good fighter. I want to see what I'm up against before I jump into anything."

Logan nodded and ordered everyone into the trees to shift. I stayed where I was and waited for them to return.

Closing my eyes, I focused on the rustling of the wind in the trees. My senses ranged out, and I could hear the quiet bubbling of the stream that seemed to run endlessly through these woods. Everyone filtered back into the clearing and I forced myself back to my feet.

I was lucky enough to find myself pairing up with Rikki. Her wolf form, much like Lee's, was a fluffy mass that looked like she belonged on a child's bed.

Everyone except Corie found a partner, and training truly began.

Chapter Twenty-Two

Logan landed on me for what had to be the hundredth time in the last five minutes.

A bone deep groan slipped free, and I shoved him off me before hobbling to my feet. His brows quirked as his tail wagged.

"*Are you doing okay, ma vie?*" he asked.

Nodding, I took a deep breath to steady myself. "*Just a little tired,*" I admitted, knowing it was useless to lie to him. He always seemed to figure me out.

He trotted over to me and nudged my shoulder, attempting to move me to the edge of the clearing. "*Go sit out for a few rounds. There's no use in beating yourself up,*" he said.

"*No,*" I argued, shaking my head before sinking into a crouch again. "*I'm fine.*"

He gave me a hard look before tackling me again. My breath left me in an audible gasp as my back collided with the hard ground.

"*Torian, take a break,*" he ordered, the slightest tinge of an Alpha's tone infecting his voice to show me just how serious he was.

"*Alright,* alright," I huffed.

"*That's my girl.*"

"You're lucky I don't kick your ass for that one," I muttered, sinking down to lie on the soft leaves near the tree line.

My eyes closed of their own accord, and I just listened to the packs. Snippets of conversation carried to me as the wolves went at each other. When I caught a piece of Rikki's and David's conversation, I couldn't help but laugh at the pair.

"C'mon, Rik," David jeered.

A dull thud sounded as Rikki tackled him.

"How's that?" she asked, laughter laced through the words.

David grunted unintelligibly in response before I heard him knock Rikki off of him. *"Good enough,"* he said, and I could almost see the smirk that would surely fit itself onto his face. *"For now."*

The sounds of woods slowly overtook out the sounds of fighting, and I slipped into the warm darkness of sleep.

The scent of burning wood wafted its way into my nose, causing me to scrunch it up. Raising my hand to my face, I rubbed my eyes to remove the sleep from them.

Hands?

"So you're a Pierce?" the unnervingly familiar voice spoke.

Sitting bolt upright on the cot, I took in the cabin as I searched for him. No matter which way I turned, I couldn't locate Xander. As I scanned the cabin again, I remembered I had been in wolf form when I fell asleep. A quick inspection let me know I was wearing the last thing Xander had seen me in, and I breathed out a sigh of relief.

"Where are you?" I asked.

"Right here," he said, seeming to materialize out of the shadows themselves with a sly grin on his face. "Miss me?"

"Not in the slightest." I swung my legs over the side of the cot, wanting to be ready to bolt at a moment's notice.

The hint of a scowl flashed across his face as he leaned against the end of the cot. He moved to sit, and I held up a hand to halt him. That liquid silver gaze met mine, and I had to admit that it was fear that skittered down my spine.

I was afraid of Xander. Afraid of all that he was capable of.

My frame quivered from the mixture of fear, anger, and exhaustion that were writhing through my body. Xander noticed, and his head cocked to the side.

"Torian, what's wrong?" And that was genuine worry lacing his tone as he knelt in front of me. "You're shaking like a leaf."

"You're what's wrong with me," I muttered, batting away the hand he reached toward me.

"What do you mean?"

My eyes widened as I gaped at him. But then I examined him a little harder. The vampire that stood before me differed from the one I was used to. His eyes were soft, and none of his signature smooth arrogance was anywhere to be found.

It's just an act, a little voice in the back of my mind whispered.

"You're starting a war," I said, exasperated, as I snapped out of the slight trance I was in. "Did you think that wouldn't affect me?"

He ran a hand through his hair, and I noticed it didn't seem like it was the first time. "Of course it would," he muttered, standing again. "But you weren't supposed to be involved."

"Did you think you'd be able to keep me separate from this?" I asked, scooting closer. He was talking. Maybe I could finally pry some information out of him.

"A fool's hope, it would seem." He settled those quicksilver eyes on me, and a small smile twisted his mouth. "He's your mate. You'll always side with him."

"That is generally how a mating bond works."

"And if I gave you a way to end the fighting. Would you take it?"

My heart stopped.

A trap, a trap, a trap-

And yet...

"What do you mean?"

"You remind me of someone. Someone I used to love *very* much, and I can't help but find myself drawn to you because of it," his admission was soft, and I had to remind myself that this was a man, a *vampire,* who had just slaughtered over half of Logan's pack. "Come with me, and I'll leave this whole feud behind."

"You were planning this long before I came along, and you expect me to believe you'd give it all up. Just like that?"

"There's more to life than land," he said with a wistful smile. "And this war, if it continues, will be brutal. I don't want you to be a part of it."

"You just killed over thirty shifters, and now you're ready to throw in the towel? That doesn't make sense..." I trailed off, my mind snagging on the first thing he had said to me today. My gaze snapped up to his. "You know my family's here."

"I do."

At least he didn't try to play dumb.

"And that scares you."

"Fighting Logan's pack is considerably easier than your family."

"I won't abandon him, not after what you've done."

"I'm not responsible for the deaths of his pack, not directly anyway," Xander said, his eyes earnest as they held mine.

"What?" I asked, incredulity dripping off the word.

"My second made a very stupid, shortsighted decision. She wasn't under my orders, but I'm sorry, all the same."

Our eyes held as Logan's voice broke through, sounding so far away.

For some reason, I believed him. And I *hated* it. But before I could open my mouth and demand more answers, the cabin faded.

But those silver eyes lingered even as I snapped back to the real world.

"Ma vie?" Logan asked softly.

My eyes fluttered and I could see him crouched in front of me in his human form. I had made it through the dream in wolf form, and I thumped my tail on the ground as I met Logan's worried gaze.

Relief washed over his features, and he pressed his brow to mine. "Thank the gods you're alright," he muttered.

Pushing to my feet, I nodded toward the trees before bolting for them. Finding my clothes was easy enough, and I prepped myself to shift back.

But before I could, I heard a twig snap not too far off.

My ears perked up, and all senses went on high alert. Scanning the trees for any sign of life, I saw the face of a woman peeking out at me. Her ebony hair framed her heart-shaped face, but it was her eyes that caught and held my attention. They were the lightest blue, like glacial chips of ice, and she watched me with cool detachment. A slow smile crept over her angelic face, fangs flashing, before she turned on her heel and took off.

She had to be with Xander.

Shifting in an instant, I yanked my clothes on before running after her. She was standing alone when I caught sight of her again, waiting. Her head cocked to the side as I came to a stop.

"Who are you, and why are you here?" I asked, keeping a fair amount of distance between us.

"Easy, Torian," she said, her voice surprisingly soft as she continued to study me. "I'm just doing my job."

"And what is that?"

"Collecting information."

Xander's words flitted through my head, and I narrowed my eyes at her. "You're Xander's second." Her brows raised, but she nodded. "You're the one who killed all those shifters."

She bristled. "Casualties are a part of war."

"You're about to be the next one."

My skin heated as I prepped to shift again, and she drew a dagger like she had planned for it.

"Raven," a deep voice snapped.

Both of our heads whipped up to the trees above us, and there he was. Xander leaned casually against the trunk of a great oak, quicksilver eyes watching every move we made. The female behind me cursed, and I felt more than saw her shift a little closer to me.

"Xander," I greeted. "What an unpleasant surprise."

A light chuckle escaped him as he dropped gracefully from the tree, landing mere feet in front of me. Taking a step back, I bumped into Raven. She ran her hands up my arms, settling them on my shoulders. My spine stiffened at the cool touch.

The hell was she doing?

"Now, now," Xander said, calling my attention back to him. "That's not very nice."

Glaring at him, I tried to steady my racing heartbeat. The last thing I needed was to pick a fight I couldn't win. If it were still just Raven and me, one on one, I *might* have a chance. But with Xander here too, I'd be fighting a losing battle.

Raven's fingers flexed, reminding me she still had them on me. I shook her off, sidestepping out from between the vampires. They kept their eyes fixed on each other, but I noticed Xander took a single step that placed him between Raven and me.

Interesting.

"What are you doing?" he asked her.

"I was scouting," she fired back, those icy eyes blazing. "Found your little she-wolf all alone and decided to say hi."

There was a threat buried in her sweet tone, and I wasn't the only one that caught it.

It happened so fast, if I would've blinked I would've missed it.

Xander lunged for her, his hand lashing out and back-handing her across the face. Her body flew backward, slamming into a tree. The tree, not being able to withstand the blow, toppled. The sound of roots ripping free from the ground resonated through the forest. It was so loud I was positive that the wolves I had left back in the clearing would hear it.

Xander reappeared in front of me, and I blinked at him as his hands hovered around my face before he dropped them back to his sides.

"Are you alright?" he asked.

"You threw her into a tree, not me. I'm fine." A low chuckle escaped him, and he gave me a small smile before stepping forward. I took an equal step back, and my back met the bark of a tree.

How cliche.

"Scared?" he taunted, invading my space. It was something he hadn't done since that first day, and the mark he had left me with pulsed as if it remembered too.

"She's the one you were talking about earlier, your second, right?" I deflected.

"She is."

"And you attacked her... why?"

"She's caused enough damage I may not be able to repair. I wasn't letting her do anything else stupid today."

Because it *had* been a threat. She thought she could manipulate Xander through me, which only meant that what he had said during the dream was true. If I was a truly a weakness, then maybe I could use it to our advantage.

"Tor!" a new voice called, cutting my thoughts off. A voice so familiar, it filled me with relief and dread all at once.

"David," I breathed, whipping my head around to meet his tawny eyes. He was barely twenty feet away, his eyes locked on the vampire who stood less than a hairsbreadth from me. Fury raged in his eyes, and I knew I had to intervene before he did something stupid. "Stay there."

My best friend just looked at me like I was crazy.

"And leave you with him again?" he asked, a glare aimed at Xander. "Not a chance."

Xander made a move toward him, and I caught his arm before he could step away from me. His eyes flicked down to mine, and I saw the predator there. The one that wasn't used to being interrupted, and that viewed David as a threat.

"Don't hurt him, Xander. You've done enough," I pleaded, my voice low. David couldn't take him on his own. I didn't know if we'd be able to take him on even together. Especially not with the brand on my neck, since I still didn't know the full scope of what it meant.

"Why?" he asked. His voice was soft, but the anger lying in wait underneath the surface was anything but.

"He's important to me," I whispered.

Xander sighed, but didn't move away from me. "On one condition," he said, something sparking in his eyes.

"Name it." Anything to keep David safe. To keep my pack safe.

"Consider it." My brows pulled together as I searched his face. Consider what?. "I will spare his life, just this once, if you promise to think about what we talked about earlier."

Leaving with him. Good gods, he was serious.

But considering it didn't mean I had to go through with it.

"Okay," I agreed. If it could hold him off for even a short amount of time, it was worth it.

A smile broke out across his face as he stepped away from me. "Until we meet again, darling," he said, tipping an imaginary hat. He launched into the trees, and then he was gone.

Chapter Twenty-Three

DAVID MADE IT TO me only a heartbeat later.

"Are you okay, Tor?" he murmured, pulling me into his warm embrace. Nodding, I returned his hug and buried my head in his shoulder.

"Fine. Where's Logan?" I asked, redirecting him so that he wouldn't question what Xander and I had discussed.

"Not far behind, and Jake's with him," he told me, pulling away just enough to hold me at arm's length. "I was already on my way to look for you when the tree cracked. Logan told everyone to stay put, but Jake just wouldn't listen-"

"Of course I wouldn't!" my brother's voice cut in as he burst through the trees. "This is my sister you're talking about," he said, pulling me into a hug of his own.

"What happened, ma vie?" Logan asked, coming up beside Jake and me.

"It was just Xander," I explained, not wanting to tell the three overprotective males that I had been alone with two vampires.

"Liar," he whispered in my ear when I wrapped my arms around his waist and cuddled into the security of his embrace.

"Okay, and the girl. Raven," I grumbled, realizing yet again lying to him was next to impossible.

"Well, at least you're safe," David said, cutting off Jake, who had been about to open his mouth.

"Let's just go back," I said, ready to put as much space between this place and myself as possible.

"It's going to rain soon anyway," Logan told us as he turned me back in the direction they had come from.

The walk back to the packs was a tense, quiet one. I knew they were all dying to figure out what really happened, but I wouldn't tell them just yet. Maybe Logan, but only because he'd inevitably get it out of me, anyway. The other two would only worry, and I needed them focused on training for now.

Ashlyn and Michael were up and running the moment they saw us slip back into the clearing.

"What happened?" they chorused.

"Vampire run in," I said before any of the males could open their mouths. "It was no big deal." The mated pair gave me a skeptical glance, but they didn't push.

"Alright," Logan called, gaining everyone's attention. "A storm's coming in. Training's over for today. You can all return to your assigned houses."

Murmurs of gratitude filtered through the clearing as everyone wearily stood. As Logan and I turned to go to the pack house, my father's voice called out, "Torian!"

"Yes?" Glancing over my shoulder, I saw him jogging toward us.

"Are you alright?" he asked when he drew close enough.

How many people were going to ask me that?

"I'm fine," I said dismissively with a wave of my hand.

"You're sure?"

"Yes."

He winced at the curt tone. "That's good."

There was an uncomfortable silence as we stared at one another. Logan, thankfully, broke it. "Mr. Pierce, I'd like to get Torian home."

Victor nodded before moving out of our way. "Of course," he mumbled as we brushed past him.

"Thank you," I whispered once we were far enough away.

"No problem," Logan responded. "You're going to tell me what really happened, right?"

"It was nothing."

"Torian."

"Yes, of course."

"Good girl," he said with a smile as we crossed into the house.

"Don't start with that," I warned.

"Yes, ma'am."

"Shut up." When I went to turn into the bedroom, Logan pulled me back to him.

"Whoa, whoa, whoa," he murmured. "Follow me." He took my hand in his and drug me farther into the house than I had ever gone.

"Where're you taking me?" I asked.

A soft laugh built in his chest as we continued walking. "Somewhere to let off a little steam," he told me, finally stopping in front of a door at the very end of the hall. He opened the door with a flourish, waving me in. With a quirked eyebrow, I stepped into the room and burst out laughing.

It was nothing more than a game room.

The oak wood pool table in the middle had plenty of room around it to play. On the opposite side of the room, an over-stuffed leather couch faced a flat screen TV. There were several gaming consoles I didn't know the names of attached to the television.

"This is pretty nice," I mused, walking straight to the couch and falling onto it.

"I've wanted to bring you back here for a while, but we keep getting distracted," he said, rubbing the back of his neck.

"We're here now." Jumping up, I crossed over to the pool table and selected a cue stick. "Wanna play?' I asked, turning to him.

"You know how to play?" he asked, surprise flashing across his face as he came to my side.

"Of course."

"Well then, show me what you've got." He racked the balls and motioned for me to break.

"With pleasure," I taunted, bending down before lining up the cue ball. Taking a deep breath, I shoved the cue stick forward.

Crack.

Two solid-colored balls fell into the pockets as Logan gaped at me.

"How?" he asked, eyes as wide as saucers.

"Jake and I used to play all the time," I said, shrugging one shoulder.

"Unbelievable," he muttered as I lined up another shot.

A smile overtook my face before I could stop it. Shaking my head slightly, I drew the stick back again before letting it connect with the cue ball. This time I missed.

Purposely, of course.

The game continued until Logan finally sank the eight ball. Rolling my eyes at him as he did a little victory dance, I replaced my stick where it went and crossed my arms over my chest.

"Would you quit already?" I asked, trying not to laugh at him.

"One more time," he said, slightly jumping into the air with his fist raised. "Now I'm finished."

"You're ridiculous," I muttered, but the smile twitching at the corners of my mouth was hard to contain. He was so excited he had beaten me, I almost wanted to tell him I had thrown the game. But I wouldn't, because that would be lying. Even though I had missed a couple shots on purpose, Logan had won fair and square when we had one striped ball and one solid left on the table.

"Maybe so," he said, ambling over to me. "But I can live with it." He passed me and flopped down onto the couch. Patting the space next to him, he sent an impish grin my way. "Come watch a movie with me."

With a quirked eyebrow, I crossed to the couch and sat down next to him. His muscular arms wrapped around me as he pulled my body against his chest. The warmth radiating from him caused me to snuggle closer, and I could almost feel his smile.

"Shut up," I muttered.

"Yes, ma vie," he said, laughter rumbling in his chest as he picked up the remote and flipped on the TV.

Chapter Twenty-Four

She was considering it.

That was all that mattered to Xander aside from the war itself.

If she was considering leaving, even for a millisecond, he had successfully broken past her barriers.

Now Xander just had to figure out how to use it to his advantage.

The thought of that tawny eyed boy from her pack caused a growl to vibrate in his chest. Looking back, the boy was the same one who had nearly saved Torian from him on that very first day. Had Torian not stopped him, Xander didn't doubt he would've killed the shifter.

One less person to get in the way in the long run.

For the first time since he had recruited her, Raven was absent from the area. He knew she had felt the blow to her pride more than the one to her cheek. She'd be back once she nursed her ego.

Something brushed against his subconscious, and he knew Torian was falling asleep. He stood and paced in front of the cot. More than anything, he wanted to bring her to him again. The image of her staring up at him in the clearing flared in his mind.

Imploring him to spare her friend as those crystalline eyes bored into his.

And then the image shifted.

The blue of Torian's eyes shifted to a teal so vibrant, it had always reminded him of the Caribbean sea. That dazzling smile he had known so well, framed by mahogany hair that had felt like silk against his fingers.

Xander couldn't breathe.

She hadn't haunted him for years. He would have thought he would have accepted what he'd done by now.

He dug his fingers into his temples, trying to control his breathing. Regret slammed into him hard enough to force him to his knees.

He reached for that connection without even realizing it. Whether or not either of them liked it, Torian's presence always acted like a balm to his fraying nerves. Her pulse pounded in his ears, the steady beat grounding him. He envisioned her there with him, drowning out the memory of one of the worst mistakes he had ever made.

In the next heartbeat, he was asleep and sharing the dream with Torian.

Her lashes fluttered, and a scowl twisted her features the moment she recognized the cabin. She sat up, her crystal eyes already searching for him.

"Right here, darling," he called, pushing to his feet. Her mocha waves fell in her face as she whipped around to face him.

"What do you want now?" Her voice sounded exasperated.

"I thought I had made that abundantly clear," he murmured, chuckling lightly as he crossed the room.

"You don't still expect me to buy that, do you?" she asked.

"Nothing to buy," he said, moving to sit next to her. She flinched away from him before recovering and steeling herself where she sat. Xander could practically watch the wall go up in front of her eyes. She was shutting herself off. "It's the truth."

"Like I haven't heard that one before," she scoffed, lowering her gaze to her hands where they lay fidgeting with the hem of her t-shirt. "Why am I really here?"

She always seemed to see through his bullshit. He'd give her that.

"I needed a distraction," he admitted. This seemed to pique her curiosity. She sat up straighter and leaned slightly forward.

"Why?" she asked.

Her genuine interest caused him to smile. He scooted back until his back pressed against the wall and crossed his legs. Torian watched him expectantly, and he could almost feel her eyes studying him.

"Regrets never leave," he told her, trying to keep the bitterness out of his voice as he focused on the ceiling. "No matter how much you try to forgive yourself for something, it's never fully gone."

"What do you regret that's weighing on you like this?"

"Logan and I have more history than you know," he said, dropping his chin in order to meet her inquisitive eyes again. "We've always hated each other, but the hatred runs deeper than we've told you."

"Would you stop speaking in riddles? What are you two hiding from me?" she asked. Her eyes searched his before narrowing.

Oh, so she had already suspected. Interesting. But Xander knew he had already said too much. He didn't want to go back to that time in his life. Even though he was dying to tell her, to get it off his chest, he couldn't make himself say the words.

He almost felt as if it wasn't his place.

"Xander?" She waved her hand in front of his face. He caught her wrist, and her dumbfounded expression caused him to grin. He expected her to rip free of his grasp, but she didn't.

Limbo. That's where they were.

"Yes?" he finally murmured, realizing she was waiting for him to speak. He brushed his thumb over the inside of her wrist, and he felt her pulse jump in answer.

"Are you going to tell me or not?" she asked, drawing in a shuddering breath as she pulled her hand back.

"Not."

"Xander." The growl in her voice made him chuckle, trying to disguise it when she sent a rather scathing glare his way.

"All in due time, darling," he told her softly, reaching out to tuck a piece of hair behind her ear.

"I hate you," she muttered, staring at him. She hadn't flinched away from his touch this time, which was an improvement. "All these secrets won't get you anywhere, you know."

As he opened his mouth to speak, the distant sound of Logan's voice carried to them. Xander gritted his teeth in frustration, but he sighed in the next instant. He always knew his timing with Torian came with an expiration tag, but this meeting had served its purpose. He felt more settled than he had only moments before.

He let the connection to Torian's dream slip from his mind. "Until next time," he purred as her pulse sang in his ears again.

When Xander opened his eyes, he was alone in the cabin.

Torian was gone.

He picked himself up from the floor where he had fallen and dusted himself off. He needed to get Torian alone, in reality. She'd press Logan harder than ever now, he was sure of it. By the next time he saw her, she could know the full truth. He didn't know how she'd react to him then. What influence he would still have with her.

Realization hit him, and he almost smacked himself. She bore his mark. He could call her to him any time he wanted. It wasn't a part of the mark he had ever experimented with, but it was an option.

Xander headed out. As it stood, he was on as good of terms with Torian as could be expected. But he needed to give her time. Even if Logan came clean by the next time they met, Xander needed to take a step back and focus on other points of this war.

For both of their sakes.

Chapter Twenty-Five

Nearly two months passed with no word from Xander.

We had the service for those we had lost without interference. We also gave the pack and their families time to truly mourn their loved ones.

In the downtime, we trained, and the three packs seamlessly meshed the longer we spent together.

The spring air was quickly warming as summer settled over the town. Logan and I had spent most of our time together, and it was getting damn near impossible to keep smothering the mate claim.

I didn't know exactly why I was still holding out, but *something* was still off with my mate. I wasn't giving in until I found the truth.

Every once in a while, I could steal away to hang out with girls and Corie. My sister had efficiently inserted herself into our group, and she fit in just fine.

Jake had taken up every minute of my time that the others hadn't, so being alone was out of the question.

Which was why I was sneaking out of Logan and I's bedroom at six in the morning.

Logan was sound asleep, his chest rising and falling evenly as I slipped into a pair of jean shorts. Taking a deep breath, I eased the door open and stepped into the hall. I winced as the door *clicked* shut behind me. When there were no sounds of discovery from the other side of the door, I expelled a *whoosh* of air and headed down the hall.

For what felt like the first time, I really *looked* at the pictures that lined the walls. A smile crossed my face as I saw the picture of Logan and Dalton as kids hugging each other. It was one of the cutest things I had ever seen. Back then, the boys might as well have been twins.

Shaking my head, I continued to study the photos that gave me an insight into Logan's past. Taking a step closer, I noticed that there were pictures missing. From far away, it wasn't as noticeable, but up close, you could clearly see the blank spaces where a frame had once hung.

A rustling sound in the room closest to caused me to speed up my pace and make a break for the door.

I didn't make it.

"Torian?" a voice called. Raising an eyebrow, I turned to face Dalton where he stood, rubbing his eyes. His shaggy hair was curled over his forehead and his sapphire eyes were red from sleep.

"What're you doing up, kid?" I asked, halting with my hand on the doorknob.

"I'm not the one sneaking out of the house before the sun even comes up," he grumbled, awareness finally settling over his features. "So, shouldn't I be asking you that question?" His eyes narrowed at me as he took a few steps forward. I held up my hands in surrender.

"You caught me, but I swear I'm not running away," I assured him when I saw the flash of apprehension in his eyes. I rubbed the back of my neck and cast my gaze toward the ceiling. "I've been a nomad for years, and I don't get much alone time anymore."

"Logan can be a little smothering," he muttered, walking into the living room.

That piqued my curiosity. "What do you mean?" I asked, trailing after him.

He stopped in his tracks before turning around to face me. He bit his lip, as if debating whether to tell me. "Let's just say Logan is extremely overprotective of the people he cares about anymore..." he trailed off, his eyes going unfocused. Whatever it was, he wasn't comfortable talking about it.

"Its fine, Dalton," I said, laying a hand on his shoulder. "You don't have to tell me."

"Thanks," he said. "Now you might want to get going. Logan usually wakes up around dawn."

Cursing under my breath, I thanked him and turned for the door.

"If he freaks out too much," I started, sticking my head back into the living room. "Tell him I'll be back around dusk."

"Yes ma'am," he said, saluting me and sounding so much like his brother, I cringed.

Stepping outside, I took in a deep breath of the fresh air. All I needed to do was decide where I wanted to go. The forest to my right looked foreboding in the pre-dawn light, but I made my way toward it. No matter how dark they could be, the woods were my home. They were where I had lived for the past seven years, and I felt safer in the security of the trees than in any house.

Except for maybe Logan's.

Shaking my head, I slipped between two pines and glanced over my shoulder. The pack house stood maybe twenty yards behind me, as still and calm as anything could be. A small smile twitched at the corners of my mouth as I turned and walked deeper into the trees.

Birds twittered above me, and I ambled through the woods on foot. I didn't want to shift just yet. It had been a long time since I had just taken a walk. The wind blew softly, rustling the leaves. A symphony of sounds grew as the creatures of the night went to bed and the critters of the day woke up.

It was a while before I sank down against the trunk of a great oak.

What was going on in my life?

Within the past few months, fate had thrown everything she could at me. I didn't know what I was doing half the time. The training for the war had lightened with the vampires' absence, but I was still on edge.

My father was a crucial factor in that. He had been trying to mend things. To rebuild the relationship we'd had when I was a kid. As much as I wanted to let it go, the memories of his betrayal still burned in the back of my mind every time I looked at him. I wasn't ready, not yet.

And then there was the mate claim. Logan had never been coy about how much he wanted me to accept it, but the closer we got, the more it took on a life of its own. And I wasn't sure I was prepared for all it entailed.

What would happen to my pack? Was I supposed to stand down as Alpha? Just become Logan's Luna? The thought made me physically ill as my body rebelled against the idea. And what about Ashlyn and Michael? Aside from David and me, they had no ties to this town. I would never ask them to give up our lifestyle to stay.

A million questions like these were constantly running through my head, causing me to live on autopilot.

I was sick of it.

The deep growl that rumbled in my chest was an echo of my frustration as it got the best of me. Stripping my tank top off, I shimmied out of the shorts I had put on as well. I shifted before my bra and underwear had even his the ground.

The familiar feeling of bone, sinew, and muscles reshaping themselves took over my body, and I squeezed my eyes shut.

Sometimes it still amazed me how much clearer everything looked when I shifted. The newly-blossoming leaves looked greener, and the wild flowers looked bolder. Shaking out my coat, I coiled my muscles and prepared to spring,

Then, I was off like a bullet.

"What do you mean, she left?" Logan seethed, glaring at his younger brother.

Dalton winced. "Chill out," he muttered, rolling his eyes. "She left okay? She said she needed some alone time. You haven't really let her have much breathing room recently."

Logan closed his eyes and let out a deep breath. Dalton was right, and he knew it, but that didn't mean he wanted to accept it.

Torian being alone out there made him uneasy. What if Xander got his hands on her? He didn't have a clue where she'd gone, so he wouldn't even know where to look for her.

Grumbling to himself, he made his way into the kitchen. He just wished she would have told him she wanted some time to herself. He would have gladly backed off and let her have it, if it was what she needed. His stomach twisted into knots as the thought of what all could go wrong swirled around inside his head.

"She's an Alpha," an obnoxiously familiar voice said. "She's perfectly capable of taking care of herself. Stop worrying," Ashlyn told him, surprising him when she laid a hand on his arm.

Logan looked down at her and attempted a smile. "If Michael went missing out of the blue, you can't tell me you wouldn't absolutely lose it."

"Alright, you got me there," she muttered, flashing him a smile before sliding onto a kitchen stool. "But Tor will be fine. And she's not *missing* per se. She told Dalton she was leaving,"

"Not helping."

"I tried."

"Calm down, guys," David said, walking into the room before crossing to the fridge. When he spoke again, he kept his voice low. "If you don't shut up, her brother is going to go scour the whole woods for her."

"I don't know what to make of him yet," Ashlyn mumbled, glancing over her shoulder toward the living room where Jake was sitting.

"Well, he means a lot to Tor, so we're kind of stuck with him," David reminded her, bringing the container of orange juice over to the island counter where she and Logan were standing.

Logan looked back and forth between Torian's best friends. "Can we get back to the matter at hand here?"

"Logan, I'm going to slap you," Ashlyn said, glaring at him. "Give her space or she's never going to accept the claim."

"Fine." He knew she was right. Torian wasn't the kind who could be caged, and that's exactly what he'd unintentionally been doing.

He was an idiot.

Rikki made her grand entrance, fire red ponytail bobbing as she flounced into the room. "Good morning, everyone!" she chirped, planting a kiss on David's cheek once she reached him.

"What's got you in such a good mood?" Logan asked her.

"She got laid," Ashlyn said, not even looking up from the juice she was pouring.

"Ashlyn!" Rikki hissed, turning the same color as her hair.

"What?" Ashlyn asked, shrugging. "There's only one thing that makes a girl glow like that. And you two weren't exactly quiet about it."

David glared at the brunette. "You're an idiot."

"But you love me," she cooed, hopping off the stool before skipping off to find her own mate.

"Can I strangle her?" Logan asked after he was sure she was out of earshot.

"No, because deep down you know you find her amusing," David grumbled in reply.

Deep, *deep* down.

Logan shoved away from the counter and ambled into another room. He didn't want to be around the love birds when he didn't even know where his mate was. As much as he didn't want to worry, he couldn't help it. She was out there on her own with Xander still on the loose.

The vampire's silence was unsettling. What was he planning?

After everything Xander had done to Logan and his family, he still wanted more. Logan still didn't know exactly what Xander wanted with Torian, but the fixation was there. Logan could see it, the same as he had the last time. Xander had gone to great lengths to hurt Logan then, so there was no telling what he was capable of with Torian.

Logan continued past the living room and into his bedroom. If nothing else, he was going for a run. It would clear his mind, at the very least. He changed into a pair of basketball shorts before making his way back to the front door. He didn't pause to talk to anyone, just let the door slam as he left.

Making a beeline for the trees, he took a deep breath. If he had to guess, he would say Torian was somewhere in their midst, running her heart out. He didn't want to invade her privacy, but he would feel better just knowing that he was in the same vicinity as she was.

He shifted the moment he lost sight of the house behind him.

It was ridiculous..

I had barely been gone half the day, and I already wanted to go back.

Huffing out my frustration, I slowly made my way back to the pack house.

But it didn't take long before I changed direction.

I couldn't explain it, but I was following my instincts as I headed in the opposite direction from the house.

The collision blindsided me.

My body hurtled into the trunk of a tree, and a low groan broke free. Shaking my head, I stood on wobbly legs and turned to glare at whatever had crashed into me.

"*Ma vie?*" Logan's voice echoed inside my head.

When my eyes met his hulking black form, I had to blink a few times to make myself believe it. "*Logan?*" I asked, hesitantly stepping closer.

He panted, teal eyes glittering as he took me in. "*Fancy meeting you here,*" he said, sitting and thumping his tail on the ground.

"*You didn't come looking for me, did you?*" I accused with an indignant huff.

"*No. I just went for a run because I was freaking out. I needed to clear my head.*"

"*I was just getting ready to go back anyway,*" I said, my eyes slipping closed as I laid down.

"Miss me too much?" he asked playfully as I heard him approach.

"Exactly," I said, deciding there was no point in lying to him. A wolfy chuckle escaped him as he laid down next to me, nudging my nose with his.

"I missed you, too." His voice was barely a murmur in my head.

Contentedness swept over me as we lay side by side. The restlessness I had felt all day evaporated the longer we spent together.

"Let's go," I finally told him, standing and shaking out my fur. I was ready to just be home.

Nodding, he rose to his feet as well and walked ahead of me. *"Alright."*

Following him, I let my brain wander. I felt safer with Logan than I did on my own, and that made me uneasy. To say I wasn't used to depending on someone else was an understatement. Even though I had agreed to quit fighting him, it didn't mean I was alright with needing him.

The edge of the trees came into view and broke my train of thought. *"I'll be right back,"* I said, trotting off to locate my clothes.

"I'll be right here," he called after me.

It didn't take long to find them, and I shifted the moment I did. I was still pulling my shirt over my head when I made it back to where I had left Logan. He was already standing there in human form, in nothing but a pair of basketball shorts. My cheeks bloomed with color as my eyes trailed down his chest.

"Can't you ever put a shirt on?" I muttered as I stopped in front of him. His laughter rumbled deep in his chest.

"You know you like it," he replied, wrapping his arms around me and pulling me into his chest.

"Whatever," I said with a smile on my face as I cuddled closer to his warmth.

He steered me toward the house. "You hungry?" he asked.

It was right about lunchtime, and just as I was about to open my mouth and answer, my stomach let out an obnoxiously loud growl.

"Answer your question?" I asked as my cheeks filled with color again.

"I'll make you something, c'mon," he told me, keeping one arm securely around my waist as the house grew closer and closer.

Jake tackled me the instant I crossed the threshold. "If you ever pull a stunt like this again, I'm going to kill you," he whispered harshly in my ear.

A giggle bubbled out of my mouth before I could stop it. "I'm sorry."

"Better be," he grumbled as he pulled away from me.

Reaching up, I patted his cheek and then walked into the kitchen. Logan was already there, pulling things out of the refrigerator. "I can make myself something," I told him, laying a hand on his arm.

"Go sit down, ma vie," he said gently, nudging me toward the table.

Putting my hands up in surrender, I did as he said. When I took my seat, I was directly in front of the sliding glass door that gave a full view of Logan's backyard. A smile fitted itself on my face as I pictured the younger versions of Logan and Dalton I had seen in the picture this morning tromping around the yard.

Logan set a plate in front of me, breaking me out of my reverie. Looking down, I saw he had made a grilled cheese that was cooked to perfection. "I might be impressed," I told him, poking at the sandwich.

"You should be. I told you I could cook." A smug smile crossed his face as he returned to the stove. "Eat."

Resisting the urge to salute him, I picked up the sandwich and took a bite. As far as grilled cheeses went, that had to be the best one I had ever tasted.

"Did you add something to this?" I asked after I had swallowed down another few bites.

"Family secret," he said with a wink.

"Kill joy," I muttered, popping the last piece of bread into my mouth.

His deep laugh reverberated off the walls. "You might learn it one day," he told me, coming over with his own sandwich and sitting down across from me. "Done already?"

"It was good," I said, shrugging.

"Do you want another one?" He was already getting up when I shook my head.

"I'm fine."

"You're sure?" He only sat back down after I vigorously nodded. He raised the sandwich to his mouth and took two bites before it was gone. I stared at him, openmouthed.

"You pig," I teased once I found my voice again.

He shrugged. "You learn to eat fast with Dalton in the house."

"I'm not that bad," the younger brother quipped, appearing directly behind me.

Startled, I whirled around in my chair. "A little warning is nice."

Dalton beamed at me before ruffling my already disaster stricken hair. "But it's not as entertaining," he said, practically skipping to the fridge.

"I hate you," I mumbled under my breath, attempting to smooth out my hair.

"Don't lie," he cooed, plopping down into the seat next to me. "You love me,"

"Maybe deep, deep, *deep* down," I told him, a smile twitching at the corners of my lips as I tried to stay serious

"Don't be mean to him," Logan inserted, coming to his brother's rescue. I was half tempted to throw something at him, but I refrained. Instead, I stuck my tongue out at him like a five-year-old.

"Coming from the bully himself," I retorted.

"I am not!"

The argument that ensued about whether Logan was a bully made me debate how old the brothers actually were. For a few moments, I just sat back and observed the two before they tackled each other. They were wrestling on the floor, and neither of them seemed to win. The entire scene would have been humorous had I not gotten dragged into it.

Dalton shoved Logan across the floor and right into my chair, causing it to topple over. The result was me lying on top of

Logan's chest. A mischievous grin lit up his face, but he eased me out of the way before I could dwell on it for too long. Dalton resumed their wrestling match, and I hoisted myself to my feet.

Only to be knocked back down again not even five seconds later.

Whipping my head around, I met Logan's eyes, which were glittering in amusement.

"Now you're in trouble," I growled, jumping toward him.

The three of us continued to roll around on the ground. A small crowd had gathered at the kitchen entrance. They were all laughing too hard to be of any help to me. Ashlyn, on the other hand, was just watching me with an irritatingly knowing look in her eyes. After a few more moments of attempting to disentangle myself from them, I sighed dramatically.

"Tired, ma vie?" Logan asked, suddenly pinning me under his weight.

"A little," I admitted with a smile. Secretly, my fingers crossed, hoping he'd let me up.

"Alright," he said easily, standing and pulling me up as well.

"And just when I was just starting to have fun," Dalton whined, still seated on the floor.

"You sound like a three-year-old," I told him.

"Whatever," he grunted as he stood.

I was just about to open my mouth when a searing pain in my neck cut me off.

Chapter Twenty-Six

CRYING OUT, I BATTED Logan's hand away when he reached for me.

Tears welled in my eyes, and I realized it was Xander's mark. It was burning as if someone was holding a red-hot iron against my skin. The heat building beneath the mark began to move and radiate throughout my entire body. My veins were on fire. The tears spilled over as I crumpled in on myself, sinking to the floor.

Logan's arms were around me in an instant. His tone was soothing, but I couldn't make out a word he was saying. Jake and David were there as well, but nothing they said was making sense, either. It was like my senses had completely shut out everything but the inferno roaring in my blood.

A restlessness started inside me. Even through the pain, something was pulling me toward the front door. Confusion settled in as I forced myself to my feet and my body began moving without my consent. I was out the door and halfway to the woods before the others could catch me.

Over and over again, I tried to stop the advance of my legs, but every attempt failed. The mark continued to pulse, sending heat waves surging through me. I couldn't think straight enough to figure out what was happening. Nothing that I knew of could make Xander's mark do this.

Xander.

The memory of Logan saying he didn't know what all bearing Xander's mark entailed flashed through my head. Cursing the vampire to the deepest pits of hell, I fought even harder against my uncooperative body.

Tears spilled down my cheeks as I sprinted through the forest. Fighting the pull was proving useless, so I gave in.

Gods above help Xander when I found him.

She was up and gone so fast, Logan didn't have a prayer of catching her.

He still tried.

But when he got to the front door and wrenched it open, Torian was nowhere in sight.

Logan slammed the door shut and rested his forehead against it.

He was failing her again, and it killed him. But whatever had happened, it had burned her scent away the same way it seemed to burn her. He couldn't track her. And without their bond in place, he couldn't use it either.

"It had to be Xander," David said, his voice grim as he came to a stop right behind Logan.

"It's the only thing I can think of," Logan replied, turning to press his back against the door.

"We have to go after her."

"How?" Ashlyn asked, coming up beside them. "Can you smell her? Sense her? Because I can't."

"I don't care," David growled, his eyes locking on Ashlyn's. "He's nearly killed her once. What if he doesn't stop this time?"

"He cares too much about her," Logan muttered, disgusted to know that his words were true. Xander may be his enemy, but he had known the vampire his entire life. And that warmth that overtook his face anytime he was near Logan's mate was real.

But then again, he had thought that before...

"Let's go," Michael said. Logan's head whipped toward the other male, who stood in the kitchen archway. Ashlyn's mate was quiet by nature, and it seemed Logan wasn't the only one who had been surprised to hear him speak. His voice had placed an almost impenetrable hush over the room. When he spoke again, it was only to his pack. "I don't care what we have to do to find her. I'm not risking losing her again."

Logan internally cringed. That tone in Michael's voice, that grim certainty, made his heart drop. How reckless had Torian been before he'd known her? Her pack was always so sure of her ability to take care of herself, and he had always assumed it was just because she was their Alpha.

But with that look on their faces, he was starting to believe it was from experience.

"Ashlyn has a point," Brooke said, easing her way into the room with Troy in tow. "How would we find her? This territory and these woods span for *miles*. Logan's connection to her is weak with the claim being unaccepted, and whatever magic is in Xander's mark erased her scent. Troy already tried tracking it. We need a *plan.*"

Troy was the best tracker Logan knew, and he swore under his breath.

Logan opened his mouth to speak, but the slamming of the sliding glass door in the kitchen cut him off. Exchanging curious glances, they all moved to the bay window in the living room.

David was rounding the house, headed straight for the woods.

It was all the incentive Logan needed.

"Dalton, Brooke," he said, already headed to the front door. He glanced over his shoulder, and his Beta and Third were waiting for his order. "Get the Pierce's together and split the area. We're finding her."

He didn't wait for their nods of approval before he took off. While everyone had valid points, he couldn't sit by and do nothing.

)))))DOCCCCC

The sun beat down on me through the gaps in the trees above.

Tears flowed freely down my cheeks as I stumbled drunkenly through the woods. The inferno in my veins intensified with every step I took. Swiping at my cheeks, I bit back another agonized scream.

Just when I thought I was going to burn alive, the pain stopped altogether.

I crumpled to my knees. My chest heaved as I fought to control my breathing. Twigs snapped in front of me, and I didn't bother looking up when two black combat boots entered my field of vision.

"Torian?" he asked, voice as silken as ever. Still refusing to look up, I just shook my head. "Hey," he murmured, fabric rustling as he knelt before me. His fingers felt like ice as they brushed my inflamed cheeks. My eyes popped open, and he was so close to me I could see the flecks of black in his quicksilver gaze. He studied me, and what looked like worry creased his brow. "What happened?"

"You don't know?" I asked, eyes narrowing. But if I was being honest, he genuinely looked confused as he used his thumb to wipe away an errant tear.

I hated how soothing that touch felt.

"Know what?"

"That whatever you just did caused me to feel like I was being burned alive."

The color drained from his face as he dropped his hands.

"I'm sorry," he said, running a hand through his hair. "I'm so sorry."

"For what, Xander?" I asked with a humorless laugh. Despite my irritation, I didn't push him away. He was knee to knee with me on the ground, and the chill emanating from his body was soothing the aftermath of the burning.

"Everything," he stated, sounding as sure as I'd ever heard him as he took one of my hands in his.

"Be a little more specific. There's a lot of shit you have to apologize for," I said, trying to pull away from him, but he held firm.

"What part of *everything* do you not understand?" he asked.

I was so tired, and I let my head drop back to look skyward. Taking a deep breath, I rolled my neck and shoulders before meeting Xander's gaze again. There was a charge in the air between us, and I couldn't explain it. I didn't know if I wanted to rend his head from his shoulders or shake some sense into him. He still needed to pay for what had happened to Logan's pack, and I *knew* that.

But it hadn't been him. He shared the blame, but it hadn't been his order.

"Where's the other one?" I asked.

"Raven hasn't been in the area for a while."

"Why?"

"It's not your concern." The snarl that erupted from me only caused him to smirk. Maybe I would end up trying to kill him. "You won't succeed," he told me.

I blinked. And then the alarm bells pealed in the back of my head.

"Telepathy," I breathed, horror spreading through me at the revelation. "You're telepathic."

"Correct." My fingers brushed against his mark as my brain spiraled. And then I felt it, the push against my subconscious. My eyes flew back up to his, and he just nodded, letting me know it had most definitely been him. "Take a breath, Torian. I'll explain."

"Why would you do that?" How did Logan and the others *not* know?

"They don't know because it's not something I advertise. Most vampires keep their abilities close to their chest. And don't worry, I have to focus in order to do it. I can't hear you unless I'm purposely trying to."

"And the mark?"

"It's a way to extend my power," he said, shrugging as he turned and stretched his legs out. "The mark focuses it and gives me access over greater distances. I don't know the exact limitation, but, for instance, I couldn't communicate with Raven right now."

"Why me?" It was a question I had asked before, but since I already had him talking, it was worth a shot.

"I told you, you remind me of someone. And I knew it would get under Logan's skin. It was a win-win for me, no matter what."

"One of you has to break and tell me the truth," I muttered, irritation with my mate flaring against my will.

Xander gave me a sad smile, shoving to his feet. Eyeing the hand that he extended like it would bite me, I finally relented and let him pull me up as well.

"It won't be me, darling," he murmured, tucking a loose strand of my hair behind my ear. "When he's ready, he'll tell you. And I'll answer any questions after."

"You could always let this feud go."

"I can't," he said. He dropped his arms to his sides and walked a few paces away from me, giving me his back.

Another impasse.

Shaking my head, I turned to head home.

"Torian..." he trailed off, bringing my attention back to him. "This is my home. I fought for it back then and lost. If it comes down to it, I will not lose again."

"Only time will tell."

He flicked his gaze back to me. "You will lose people. Your pack may die."

It was a warning, that much I knew. And an offer. If I wouldn't leave *with* him, he still wanted me to leave. To spare me and mine.

But I was in too deep.

"I will fight," I told him.

He opened his mouth, but abruptly shut it. The rest of the world trickled in, and I realized how focused on him I had been. The surrounding woods had gone eerily still, and a distant series of snapping twigs and underbrush shattered the silence.

"Tor!" I heard David yell, his voice still distant.

Xander and I stared at each other, and he brought his index finger to his lips. A quiet kind of rage danced across his features, and fear for my friend seized my heart.

I turned on my heel and ran.

At least I tried. Xander's arm snaked around my waist and used my own momentum to slam me back into him.

David broke through the tree cover in front of us not even a second later, and his eyes locked on Xander. Hatred overrode all common sense on his face, and David lunged.

Xander pushed me behind him, but it was unnecessary. David landed, fully shifted, a few feet in front of us, snarling as his hackles rose from the back of his neck to the base of his tail. Xander bared his teeth, fangs gleaming in the sunlight.

"Not him," I breathed, knotting my fingers in the hem of his t-shirt. Xander tilted his head just enough to let me know he'd heard me, but he didn't take his attention from David for a second. "Xander, please. Not him."

He's going to attack the second you're in the clear, Xander's voice floated through my mind like a caress. My heart stuttered in shock.

Glad to know he could *implant* thoughts as well as read them.

"David, stand down," I said, stepping to Xander's side.

The wolf in front of us blinked, absolute confusion flashing across his face. Xander chuckled from beside me, and I threw an elbow into his gut.

He's still going to do it. If he attacks me, I'm not holding back. I've been itching for a fight.

I glared at the vampire beside me, and he had the audacity to smirk at me. "Go fight one of your fucking newborns," I hissed before turning my gaze back to my Beta. "Stand. Down."

The Alpha's order rang clear in my voice, and David's entire body relaxed.

"What the hell?" a familiar voice asked.

My head whipped to the side, and the first thing I noticed was the color leeching from Logan's face. His teal eyes shuttered as they surveyed the scene in front of him.

Have fun with that, Xander's voice had laughter laced through it even in my head. His lips brushed my cheek, and then he was gone.

I was going to kill all three of them.

Chapter Twenty-Seven

Both men just stared at me.

I stared back.

Gods, this had to look bad.

Growling, I shifted. Logan could wait. David needed my explanation more than him.

"*What the* fuck, *Tor?*" David asked the moment I was on all fours.

"*He knew you were going to attack him. You cannot take him on your own.*"

"*We could have-*"

"*I didn't know Logan was so close behind you,*" I said, cutting him off. Out of the corner of my eye, I saw Logan shift as well. "*Even the three of us may have struggled to take him on, and that's even if I was able to fight with this thing on my neck. I wasn't letting you risk your life because you weren't thinking straight.*"

We glared at each other, and Logan came up beside me. Gently, he knocked his shoulder into mine.

"*That makes more sense than what it looked like,*" he said, breaking the tension that had mounted between David and me.

My eyes rolled, but I refocused on David. *"You know I don't use my orders lightly. But he was going to kill you if you attacked. I wasn't letting that happen."*

"How do you know that?" David asked, eyes narrowing. *"He didn't say a word."*

Shit.

"He's telepathic."

Both men cursed, and I couldn't disagree with them.

Logan growled before shaking his head. *"Let's get home. We can talk about this later."*

As we traipsed through the woods, I tried to keep my mind off the mercurial vampire. But with everything going on, it was hard. Especially when I knew that he and the man at my side were hiding something in their shared pasts that explained their disdain for one another.

Outside of the obvious.

But the truth of it was, that secret was the only thing holding me back from accepting the mate claim.

With the start of a plan brewing in my head, I trailed after the other two wolves.

Logan and I sat at the kitchen island the next morning, both of us lost in our own heads.

I needed information, and I didn't know who to get it from. Dalton wouldn't budge. Something told me Kenna and

Nicholas wouldn't be much help either. Who else had enough dirt on the man beside me and might let it slip?

Sitting up straighter in my chair, I twisted to look at Logan. He quirked a brow at me before taking a sip of his coffee.

"Can we go see Millie?" I asked.

Suspicion immediately danced across his face. "Sure, but why?"

"Have you seen her since the attack?"

"No," he muttered, setting his eyes downcast. Regret twisted my stomach for using his own guilt against him, but I needed to know. "It probably is a good idea."

"I have those, you know."

His laughter warmed my heart, and he grabbed my hand and towed us back to the bedroom. We were dressed and ready to go in less than twenty minutes. We headed for the front door, and I caught sight of Ashlyn in the living room. She motioned for me to stop, and I complied as she disentangled herself from Michael's lap.

"Where are you off to?" she asked once she had reached us.

"Fresh air," I said, shrugging. "You should try it sometime."

Her eyes rolled so far I almost feared they'd get stuck. "Maybe I'll go for a run later."

"Take David," I said, glancing at where he and Rikki lay snuggled on the couch. "I think he's still mad at me."

"He'll get over it. His pride just took a little hit since you didn't think he could take the vampire."

"Ash, none of us could take Xander solo."

"I know that, and so does he. He'll come around."

Logan tugged on my hand. "Millie should be opening soon."

"Catch you later, Ash," I called over my shoulder. She waved before the door fell shut behind us, cutting her off from my line of sight. Focusing my attention on the town, I allowed Logan to lead me as we made our way to Millie's.

"What's going on in that mind of yours, ma vie?" Logan questioned as we reached his great aunt's shop.

"Just trying to decide what parts of your childhood to grill her about."

He groaned, pushing the door open for me. "She's worse than Mom. How did you know she'd be the one with the gossip?"

Jackpot.

"Just a good guess."

The familiar tinkle of the bell caused Millie to poke her head up from behind the counter. "Logan! Torian!" she cried, rushing around it to meet us. The strength she used to pull me into a crushing hug took me by surprise, but I hugged her back with everything I had.

"Hi, Millie," I said, laughing lightly.

"What brings you two here?" she asked, releasing me only to yank Logan into her arms.

"It's been a while," he told her, a small smile pulling at his lips. "We figured we'd come check in."

She looked suspiciously at the two of us. "I'm old, not stupid. What's with the surprise visit?"

Logan blew out a breath and looked to me for help. I just shook my head at him, trying to hide my grin behind my hand.

"How're you holding up?" he asked, his tone softening.

"I've been better," she said, understanding dawning over her face. "I knew almost every shifter that was killed. And if I didn't personally know them, I knew their family. It's been rough."

"I'm sorry we didn't come sooner," Logan murmured, taking her hand in his.

"Oh, mon garçon, I'll be okay."

My ears perked up at the way her voice lilted over the foreign words. Logan noticed, and a smug little smile played over his mouth. He inclined his head toward Millie, and I almost vibrated with excitement.

If nothing else, I was going to solve one mystery today. At least, if my assumption was right.

"What was that you just said?" I asked.

"What? Mon garçon?"

"Yes," I replied, nodding eagerly.

"Oh, it means 'my boy' in French," she said with a wave of her hand.

French.

Just like that godsdamn nickname. I had almost forgotten about wanting to figure it out. It had stopped bothering me a long time ago, but now that the answer was possibly right in front of me?

"Do you know anything else?"

"I'm nearly fluent," she told me. "I took it in school and never forgot what I learned. I've kept up with it over the years as well. Why do you ask?"

"Do you know what 'ma vie' means?" I asked, nearly shaking with anticipation.

"That's simple enough," she said. "It means *my life*."

My eyes widened as I spun to face Logan.

His life.

That's what he had been calling me from the moment he knew we were mates?

Since the first moment we had lain eyes on each other, Logan had been adamant that this wasn't a mistake. It was something he had told me time and time again.

And yet, somehow, *this* was what drove that home for me.

"Logan…" I trailed off, traitorous tears brimming in my eyes.

"Yes, ma vie?" he murmured. His smile was slow, but once it overtook his face, he could have lit every major city in the continental U.S. for a year.

Millie gasped softly, but I barely heard it as I threw myself into his arms. They tightened around me, crushing me to his chest.

"I don't even know what to say," I said, my voice muffled.

"Say that you'll never leave me," he whispered in my ear.

And it wasn't even a question.

"Never," I swore, pulling back to meet those teal eyes I loved so much.

Home. Logan *was* my home.

And with that realization, the bond snapped into place.

Chapter Twenty-Eight

So much for holding off until I knew the full truth.

A ragged gasp tore free as instant euphoria rushed through my veins. My head spun, and I tried to get a handle on myself as I *felt* my soul tie itself to Logan's.

His hold on me tightened even further, until I wasn't sure if my shortness of breath was from his grip or the magic's.

Logan watched me with a knowing gaze, eyes glittering. The minute my breathing returned to normal, he covered my lips with his and my heart flew right back into overdrive. What could have been hours, minutes, or even seconds later, I had to tear myself away from him for air. Our chests rose and fell rapidly, yet still in sync.

"Would you two stop before you make an old woman have a heart attack?" Millie chided, breaking through our moment.

"Yes, ma'am," we chorused. Both of us laughed as we turned to her.

"Now, come on upstairs. I'll make lunch." She was already moving to the back of the store.

Once she was out of sight, I raised an eyebrow at Logan. "She owns the apartment above the shop," he said, pointing to the ceiling. "Let's go."

We hastened after Millie to find her tapping her foot impatiently. "Come along then," she said, rolling her eyes as she disappeared up a flight of stairs.

"She's so bossy," Logan muttered.

"Heard that!" she called. Even though I tried not to, I couldn't help the laughter that burst out of me at the bewildered look on his face.

"Nice going," I said as I brushed past him and continued up the stairs. When I reached the top, I found myself in a one-room flat. A small kitchenette sat in the far corner with what looked like a hand carved dining set off to the side. Closer to me, there was an overstuffed couch, a coffee table, and an older model television.

"I know it's not much, but it does for things like this," Millie said, making her way into the kitchen area.

"It's cozy," I said, walking over and falling onto the couch. "I like it."

"You'll have to come by the house sometime."

"Oh, she will," Logan answered for me, sinking down beside me. Millie rolled her eyes before setting herself busy bustling around the kitchen.

"Did she teach you French?" I asked, lacing my fingers with his.

"What little I know of it." His eyes trailed down to where I held his hand. Something like wonder washed over his face, and he lifted our hands so he could place a kiss against the inside of my wrist.

"I think it's sweet that you two are this close."

"It's because I don't have any grandparents," he said, his voice soft. "So, she stepped in as one."

"C'mon, kids!" the woman in question called. We stood and made our way over, each of us taking a seat as she sat out a plate of sandwiches. "This is the best I could come up with on such short notice."

"This is perfect," Logan assured her, taking two for himself.

After I took one as well, Millie sat down and filled me in on everything about Logan's childhood.

Exactly what I had initially planned on.

It was like opening the family photo albums. She told me stories of him and Dalton when they were boys, all the trouble they would get into. With every new story she told me, his face would flush beet red. Each one just made my smile bigger.

"And there was this one time he and Trisha-"

"Torian, I think it's time we got back to the house, don't you?" Logan asked, cutting her off mid-sentence.

"What?" I exclaimed, rounding on him.

"It's getting late," he pointed out, nodding toward the darkening sky that was visible through the window above the sink. "And we have some news to share."

"I don't think-"

"Ma vie, let's go," Logan snapped, silencing me as he stood.

It was so unlike him. For a moment, all I could do was stare. The cold look in his eyes was foreign.

This was it. Whatever had set him off was what I had come here for. I was sure of it.

But I forced my muscles to move and stood as well. "It was great to see you again, Millie."

"Come back anytime. But will you please excuse Logan and me for a moment?" she asked, her eyes darting to him before they hardened.

))))))OO(((((

"You haven't told her about Trisha?" Millie snapped at Logan once Torian was well out of earshot.

"She hasn't asked, and she doesn't need to know," he told his great aunt, his voice cool.

"She has every right to know," Millie growled.

"Why would I bring that up now?" he asked, crossing his arms over his chest. "She has so much on her plate as is. She doesn't need the burden of my past on her as well."

"Tell her," she ground out, narrowing her eyes.

"In time."

"Sooner would be better than later. Keeping this from her is going to blow up in your face, mon garçon."

Logan sighed, running a hand through his hair. "I don't know *how* to bring it up to her."

"Well, you better figure it out, and quickly," she scolded, folding her arms over her chest.

"Yes, ma'am," he muttered, knowing she was right. If Torian were to learn he had been keeping Trisha a secret, he knew it wouldn't end well.

The sound of the bell in the shop caused the pair to whip their heads up. Millie's eyebrows furrowed. "Did she just..."

"Leave?" Logan growled, already making his way to the door leading down into the store. "More than likely."

Back on the first floor, Logan's eyes scoured every rack, but Torian was nowhere in sight. Cursing under his breath, he stalked toward the front door. As he passed the counter, a post-it with handwriting that didn't belong to Millie caught his attention. He picked it up, already suspecting what he'd find.

Logan,

Alone time needed. I'll be back tonight. Don't worry about me.

- Torian

Logan let out another string of profanities as he crumpled the piece of paper in his hand. Damn her. He knew this was his fault, but worry pounded through him.

"Where did she go?"

"She didn't say," he grumbled, tossing the note into the small trashcan behind the counter.

"Are you going to go after her?"

"No. I know Torian, and that would only irritate her. She's an Alpha. She can take care of herself," he said, finding himself reiterating the words her pack had uttered to him time and time again.

Millie hummed. "You're probably right. I'm sure she'll be fine. Just go home and wait for her."

"Thank you for having us for lunch," he said, leaning forward to kiss her cheek.

"Anytime," she replied, shooing him out the door. "Now go."

With one last smile sent over his shoulder, he left the shop and made his way back to the pack house. Halfway there, he stopped dead in his tracks. Torian had accepted the mate claim, which meant their connection was strong enough for him to track her. He almost felt like collapsing in relief, but he held himself together.

He was just about to go after her when he stopped himself. He'd be able to tell if she was in danger. Knowing that she wanted to be on her own for the time being, he promised himself he wouldn't go looking for her unless she was in trouble.

With a heavy sigh, he continued on his way back to the house.

Logan's shocked face when he walked into the bedroom was priceless.

"I thought you needed alone time?" he asked, pushing the door closed behind him.

"I did," I said, turning so I was staring at the ceiling. He climbed into bed next to me, close but not touching.

Déjà vu rolled over me, and I could barely restrain the smile that tried to form.

We'd come full circle.

"And now?" he prompted, slipping his hand into mine and entwining our fingers.

"Now, I've realized I just need to trust you enough to ask you my questions outright." I leaned up, resting my weight on one elbow as I gazed down into his beautiful teal eyes. "Because you'd never lie to me, right, Logan?"

"Of course not," he assured me, but that was trepidation waltzing across his face.

"Who's Trisha?"

TO BE CONTINUED

Acknowledgements

Howls of the Lost was the first story I ever finished. I was a freshman in high school when I completed the very first draft. It doesn't exist anymore, even on wattpad. Sorry! But I then rewrote it my senior year, and hadn't touched it since.

In the wake of publishing my debut novel *Death of Me,* I wanted to get something else out by the end of the year. And there *Howls* sat. Just waiting for a little polishing.

With less than a month until release, I started editing.

And then said 'fuck it' and just started rewriting it.

The copy you have in your hands is arguably *drastically* different from the version so many read on my wattpad profile for the first time. If this is your first venture into this world, welcome! I hope you enjoyed it. If you've read it before, you might notice one major difference.

I'm warning you now, he's not safe.

And back to what this part is really for: acknowledgements.

Thank you to everyone who supported me in those early years on wattpad, It truly means the world to me.

Thank you, to my dear friend Cortney, who was sending me edits until the absolute deadline for submission.

And thank you, dear reader, for giving me and this story a chance.

I love you all.

About the Author

Erin Jacobs has loved storytelling for as long as she can remember. It has been her dream to craft stories that stick with people since the first time she put a story to paper when she was eight years old. She currently resides in Ohio with her child and dog, and is working on the next installment of her debut series set in fictitious Valarian City.

Stay tuned for updates on Valarian City's resident golden retriever. He's about to have his world turned upside down by a black-cat woman with a badge.

TikTok: @.aiiry

Instagram: @xoxoaiiry

Stay up to date with Erin's website:
https://erinjacobsbooks.com/